"You could show m[...]

She knew it was a [...]
care. She needed to convey her feelings, especially
with how easily they were touching each other. "I've
been wondering what your bedroom is like."

"That's a dangerous thought, Meagan."

"I can't help it." She looked into the depths of his
eyes, nearly losing herself in them. They were the
deepest, darkest, richest shade of brown, with tiny
amber flecks that she hadn't noticed before now.
"What have you been wondering about?"

"What it would feel like to kiss you."

"That's easy to find out." Meagan lifted her chin,
inviting him to satisfy his curiosity.

Garrett hesitated, but only for a moment. Clearly,
his willpower was at the brink. He tugged her even
closer, lowered his head and put his lips warmly
against hers.

Holy. Heaven. On. Earth.

Everything inside her went wonderfully weak.

***

Single Mom, Billionaire Boss is part of the
Billionaire Brothers Club series—
Three foster brothers grow up, get rich...
and find the perfect woman.

Dear Reader,

Meagan Quinn, the heroine of this book, has a two-year-old daughter named Ivy, and I wanted to give Ivy a shining little voice befitting her character.

When my son was a toddler, he struggled to speak as a result of chronic ear infections. We took him to speech therapy and eventually he developed beautifully in that regard. But as a two-year-old, words escaped him. I didn't know my stepdaughter when she was a toddler, so I couldn't model Ivy's speech after either of my children.

Just about the time I began working on this book, a mother and her young son were in line ahead of me at a retail store. After listening to his wonderful chatter, I asked her how old he was. The answer: he'd just turned two. I told her about my research, and she happily shared more information about him. As easily as that, I had a "voice" for Ivy.

Just so you know, Meagan and Ivy (who was too young to talk then) appeared in other books of mine. They were secondary characters in *The Bachelor's Baby Dilemma* and *Coming Home to a Cowboy*, published by Harlequin Special Edition in 2015. Garrett Snow, the hero of this book, was a secondary character in *Waking Up with the Boss*, my Harlequin Desire from August 2016.

Love and hugs,

Sheri WhiteFeather

SHERI
WHITEFEATHER

SINGLE MOM,
BILLIONAIRE BOSS

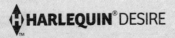

Recycling programs
for this product may
not exist in your area.

ISBN-13: 978-0-373-83822-6

Single Mom, Billionaire Boss

Copyright © 2017 by Sheree Henry-WhiteFeather

Printed in U.S.A.

Sheri WhiteFeather is an award-winning, bestselling author. She writes a variety of romance novels for Harlequin and is known for incorporating Native American elements into her stories. She has two grown children who are tribally enrolled members of the Muscogee Creek Nation. She lives in California and enjoys shopping in vintage stores and visiting art galleries and museums. Sheri loves to hear from her readers at sheriwhitefeather.com.

Books by Sheri WhiteFeather

Harlequin Desire

Marriage of Revenge
The Morning-After Proposal

Billionaire Brothers Club

Waking Up with the Boss
Single Mom, Billionaire Boss

Harlequin Special Edition

Family Renewal

The Bachelor's Baby Dilemma
Lost and Found Husband
Lost and Found Father

Visit her Author Profile page at Harlequin.com, or sheriwhitefeather.com, for more titles.

One

At twenty-seven, Meagan Quinn was starting her life over. People often said they were going to, especially screwups like herself, but she meant it.

Really, truly meant it.

She'd spent nearly three years in prison for a crime she'd stupidly committed. She'd only been out for a week, and now here she was at the Ocean Cliff Hotel and Resort, preparing to finalize the details of her employment.

She exited her car and smoothed the front of her skirt, anxious about her appearance, hoping that she looked more composed than she felt. As she crossed the parking lot, a Southern California breeze stirred her long, straight dark hair and rustled the scarf attached to her blouse.

One of the terms of her release was that she had to have a job lined up, but this one hadn't come easily. The parole commission had considered the job carefully before they'd approved it because Garrett Snow, the billionaire who owned the resort and had offered to hire her, was one of Meagan's victims. She'd embezzled sixty thousand dollars from Garrett and his equally rich foster brothers. Basically, she'd nabbed twenty grand from each man from the accounting firm where she used to work.

A portion of her wages from this job would be used for restitution so she could pay back what she'd stolen. Her victims had arranged for it to go to their foster care charity, instead of it being returned directly to them. Regardless, Meagan wanted to make amends, to prove that she was reformed.

When Garrett had offered her this job, it had been through a written correspondence, simply stating that he was willing to give her a fresh start, if the parole commission agreed that she was ready to be released. But she still wasn't sure why Garrett had decided to help her to begin with. That part wasn't quite clear to her.

She just wished that she wasn't so darned nervous about coming face-to-face with him again. She'd done him wrong, and now she was at his mercy, trying to keep her heart from blasting its way out of her chest and splattering her pretty new blouse.

Meagan entered the hotel, clutching her purse and a manila envelope that contained her paperwork. She would be working here as a stable hand. The resort offered all sorts of luxuries, including horseback riding along the beach.

As she passed through the lobby, her boots sounded on the colorfully tiled floor. The overall decor consisted of painted woods, breezy fabrics and Native American accents. Garrett was a half blood from the Northern Cheyenne Nation. Meagan had the same tribal affiliation.

She headed down the hallway that led to Garrett's office and came to two big double doors. After taking a deep breath, she opened them and approached the male receptionist seated at a circular desk. He was young and trendy, maybe a college student, with buzz-cut blond hair and a neatly trimmed beard. He greeted her with a smile, and she gave him her name. He checked her appointment on the computer and instructed her to wait.

Meagan glanced around. The waiting area was big and bright, with magazines scattered on glass-topped tables. She sat on the edge of a printed sofa and placed the envelope on her lap, trying not to fidget. She was the only person there.

About ten minutes later, the receptionist escorted her to Garrett's private office and left her alone with him, closing the door with a soft and scary click.

Garrett gazed across the room at her, but neither of them spoke. He was standing beside his desk, dressed in a sharp gray suit and Western-style boots. His short black hair was combed straight back, making the angles of his handsome face more prominent. He was a well-built man, tall in stature, with wide shoulders. By now, he would be thirty-two years old.

The last time she'd seen him in person had been at her sentencing, and that was almost three years ago. She'd broken down and cried that day, apologizing for what she'd done, but he'd been unmoved by her tears. She remembered how stoic he'd looked then. He looked stoic now, too. She wasn't even sure why he was helping her now.

Finally he said, "Have a seat."

She thanked him and took the proffered chair.

He walked behind his desk. After a moment of silence, of squaring his shoulders and straightening his tie, he sat down, too. "Did you bring the forms?"

"Yes." She handed him the envelope, hating how awkward this was.

While he sifted through the papers, she thought about how they'd become acquainted. On occasion, she'd caught sight of his foster brothers at the firm, slipping in to meet with their accountant. At the time, she hadn't yet seen Garrett, who was rumored to have a hard-edged nature. But she'd preferred it that way. By then, Meagan had already been stealing from all three men, and the last thing she'd wanted was to grow fond of any of them.

She and Neil, her longtime boyfriend, had plotted every aspect of the embezzlement, with Meagan taking the money so they could live a more glamorous life. But, in actuality, it was Neil who craved fancy things. Meagan, idiot that she was, just wanted Neil to love and adore her in the same blind-faith way that she'd loved and adored him.

Then, one day during her lunch hour at work, she

came into contact with Garrett. She was sitting on the curb outside of the building, crying, on the heels of a telephone argument with Neil.

Garrett had approached her and asked if she was okay. She'd insisted that she was, but he'd plopped down beside her anyway, introducing himself and giving her the handkerchief from his pocket. It had seemed like something out of a movie, so gallant, so old-fashioned. The hard-edged billionaire was more human than she could have imagined.

He'd walked her back inside, and while they were saying goodbye in the lobby, he'd pilfered a daisy from one of the flower arrangements and presented it to her. She remembered clutching the fragile bloom and feeling horribly guilty about the money she'd already taken from him. And when she went home that night to Neil, Garrett Snow had been all she could think about.

She'd seen him a number of times after that, and every time he came to the accounting firm's office, he stopped by her desk to talk to her, treating her like a friend.

But she wasn't his friend. She'd stolen from him and allowed Neil to burn through the money, telling herself that she'd done it because she loved Neil. Yet, even in the midst of that supposed love, she'd been fighting warm and stirring feelings for Garrett.

He glanced up from the documents in his hands. "I'll send these over to HR later today, and you can start next Monday."

"Thank you." She tried for a smile, wishing that he would smile, too. Then again, maybe it was better that he was being so detached. His smile used to make her knees watery and weak. "I really need this job."

"I'm aware of your situation." He returned the paperwork to the envelope. "I heard that you had a baby while you were in prison, and that she's about two now."

"Yes, I have a sweet little daughter." Meagan had discovered that she was pregnant soon after she was incarcerated, throwing her already-damaged world for a loop. "Her name is Ivy."

"One of your brothers took custody of her, didn't he?"

Meagan nodded. "Yes. Tanner, and his fiancée, Candy, raised her while I was in prison. There was no one else who was willing or able to take her." Feeling ashamed, she paused before explaining, "Neil wasn't an option. He walked out on me before she was born. He's never even met her."

Garrett frowned. "Why didn't you implicate Neil in the crime when the cops suspected that he'd been involved?"

She answered as honestly as she could, hating how naive it was going to make her sound. "When I first got arrested, I thought that he would remain loyal to me if I protected him. I truly believed that he would wait for me."

Garrett didn't reply. Did he think she was a fool for trusting Neil? Or did he think she deserved it?

She explained further. "I told the police that Neil was under the impression that I'd come into the money through an inheritance. That was a lie, of course. He knew I'd embezzled it. He was involved from the start. But since there was no evidence against him, he was never charged with anything." She quickly added, "I'm grateful that Tanner was there. After Ivy was born, he and Candy used to bring her to visit me. It wasn't the same as seeing her every day, but it was better than not seeing her at all." Meagan had battled her insecurities, clinging to the future, desperate to form a stronger bond with her child. "I'm trying to make up for lost time and be the best mom I can be. My baby girl is just the most amazing kid."

Once again, Garrett didn't say anything.

But she prattled on. "Tanner was nervous about taking her at first because he was single then. He didn't become engaged until later. Of course now Ivy is really close to him and Candy. I even…" She stopped midsentence.

"You what?" he asked, prodding her to finish.

"Nothing." She couldn't bring herself to admit that she'd been so distraught and depressed in prison that she'd tried to talk Tanner and Candy into adopting Ivy. But thankfully they'd encouraged her to hold tight, knowing that she didn't really want to give up her baby.

Garrett leaned back in his chair, watching her with a taut expression. Whatever he was thinking or feeling didn't seem favorable.

She gazed across the desk at him. "I'm so sorry for what I did to you. And to your foster brothers."

His expression didn't change. "You already apologized at the sentencing."

"I know. But I wanted to say it again. Here and now."

She paused, a lump catching in her throat. "I was sorry at the sentencing, too, but I didn't understand who I was then." She was a different person today. Meagan had been to hell and back. "I've grown up. I've learned from my mistakes, and if I could take it back, I would."

"Yes, but you can't. What's done is done."

She sensed that he wasn't talking about the money but the callous way he'd been treated as the entire scenario unfolded. As wrong as they were, she couldn't explain her actions, not without delving into deeper issues, including her mixed-up attachment to him.

"You're right," she said. "I can't change it."

He nodded, and they both went quiet, the past stirring uncomfortably between them.

Then, after another beat of heart-shredding silence, she asked, "Why did you offer me this job?"

He shifted in his seat. "I stated the reason in the letter I sent to you. The same letter I submitted to the parole commission."

"Yes, I know. You claimed that you wanted to give me a second chance. But you don't seem like you really want to."

"Truthfully, none of this was my idea. My mom suggested it. She's the one who convinced me to hire you."

"Your real mom or one of your foster moms?" Meagan knew that he'd once been a foster child. But she didn't know much more than that.

"My real mom. She's always been part of my life, even when she wasn't able to take care of me. But that's a whole other story."

And one he seemed reluctant to share. "Why would your mom want to go to bat for me?"

"She saw you at the sentencing and felt bad for you, with the way you were crying and whatnot."

"Was she the lady who was sitting next to you?" Now that Meagan thought about it, she recalled an older woman who could have been related to him.

"Yes, that was her. So, anyway, later on, when you were coming up for parole, she did a little research on you. I guess you could call it a background check of sorts. She was curious to know more about you, and that's when she found out that you'd had a baby."

"So this is because of Ivy?"

"Your child's welfare is part of it."

So what was the rest of it? she wondered. Apparently, there were a lot of things he wasn't inclined to discuss. Regardless, she appreciated his mother's support. Meagan's mom had died a while back, and she missed her terribly. "Do you know that my mother is gone? That I lost her before any of this happened?"

"Yes." He didn't offer his condolences, but he spoke a little more softly. "It came up in the background check."

She struggled to blink away her emotions. "Will you tell me how I can contact your mom? I'd like to thank her for convincing you to hire me." Without this job, Meagan wouldn't have gotten paroled. "Maybe I can send her a card or something?"

Garrett shook his head. "I'll relay the message."

Clearly, he didn't want her associating with his mom, even if it was just to say thanks. But she could hardly blame him. Meagan was fresh out of prison, trying to prove that she could be trusted. She certainly wasn't going to press the issue.

"We have a day care center and an after-school program here for the children of our employees," he said, changing the subject.

"Is that something that will be available to Ivy?"

"Yes, absolutely. It's free, so it won't affect your income." He removed a sheet of paper from his desk drawer and handed it to her. "Here's more information about it. If you want to bring your daughter to the day care, just call them directly to arrange for her enrollment."

"Thank you." She folded the paper and slipped it into her purse. And when she glanced back up at Garrett, she noticed how intently he was gazing at her. Sometimes she used to wonder if he'd been as attracted to her as she'd been to him. If some of those confusing feelings had been mutual.

But none of that mattered now, she reminded herself. Meagan was only here to make a living and pay back the money she owed, not to rekindle her crush on Garrett.

"I'll be a good employee," she said, needing to reaffirm her intentions out loud. "I'll work hard."

A muscle in his jaw flexed. "I'm counting on it."

Yes, of course. He was expecting her to toe the line. Her parole officer was expecting the same thing. So was Meagan's family. She had a lot of people counting on her to make the right choices from now on.

She contemplated the position he'd offered her. "Can I ask you something?"

He nodded warily. Did he think her question was going to be personal?

She closed the latch on her purse, realizing that she'd left it open. Then she asked, "What made you decide on me being a stable hand? Is it because both of my brothers work in the horse industry, and you figured that I had knowledge of it, too?"

"That's pretty much it." He squinted at her. "Why? Do you have reservations about the job? Because you told the parole commission that you were qualified for it."

"My experience with horses was a long time ago, when I was a kid. I can still do the job, though. It won't be a problem."

He angled his head. "Are you sure?"

"I'm positive." She would be feeding, grooming and saddling the animals, as well as cleaning and maintaining the stalls and equipment. "I know what it entails." And she would bust her hump if she had to. "But I just thought I should tell you that my experience was limited to when I was younger."

While she waited for him to respond, she tried not to get intimidated. Especially with how drawn to him she'd once been. And still was, she thought.

"All right," he said. "I can give you a tour of the stables now if you'd like."

"Thank you. That would be great. I'm looking forward to seeing them."

He stood and removed his jacket, and her pulse

zipped a bit too quickly. She needed to focus on her job and not on how he made her feel. She was going to work here, but she wasn't going to fall for Garrett again. She'd hurt him—and herself—enough already.

The stables were located on a grass-topped hill that overlooked the resort, with brush-lined trails leading to the beach. There were public paths that went into the hills, and beyond those trails, even higher up, on a private and gated road, was Garrett's house. This was his world, his sanctuary, and now he was lending it to a woman who'd played him for a fool.

According to his mother, he needed to forgive Meagan, to give her a chance to prove herself. Mom had all sorts of do-gooder reasons for believing it was the right thing to do.

Garrett had spent months thinking it through, and even now, he wasn't sure why he'd given in. Maybe it was because somewhere deep down, he wanted to believe that Meagan was capable of being reformed. Or maybe it was because she had a child to care for, and Garrett had a soft spot for kids.

He just wished that his mom had never dragged him into this mess. But she didn't know that he'd had romantic feelings for Meagan. No one knew, not even his foster brothers. To them, she was just someone who'd worked at their accountant's office.

But, to Garrett, she was someone he'd wanted to explore on a deeper level. If she'd been single, he would have asked her out. But since she was tied up with Neil, he'd been careful not to overstep his bounds. Of course, he'd been hoping that she was on the verge of leaving her loser boyfriend, the jerk who'd made her cry on the phone that first day, giving Garrett a chance to dash in like the knight he'd imagined himself to be.

A knight who'd gotten his armor crushed.

As they entered the barn, he glanced over at her. She was as beautiful as he remembered, with her almond-shaped eyes and long silky hair. She did seem more mature, though, far less flighty than before. Prison had changed her. Motherhood, too, he supposed. But were those changes he could trust? She might have become more conniving over the years, more charming, more of a seductress. Her sweet little apologies could be an act, and a damned good one at that.

He intended to keep a close eye on her. There was no way he was going to let her screw him over again.

Garrett spotted Tom Lutz, the barn manager, and motioned for him to come over and meet Meagan. Tom was a friendly old cowboy, short and stocky, with a big bushy mustache like the one Wyatt Earp used to wear. Once Meagan started working here, Tom would be her supervisor.

The introduction went well. Tom was his usual pleasant self, and Meagan was as sweet and humble as she'd been with Garrett back in his office. He sure as hell hoped it wasn't an act.

After a bit of chitchat, the old cowboy returned to work, leaving Garrett and Meagan alone once again.

"Tom seems really nice," she said.

"Yeah, he's as loyal as they come. He knows about your criminal history. I discussed it with him ahead of time. But he isn't going to hold it against you. The only thing that matters to him is that you do your job."

"Do the other employees at the stables know?"

"I haven't told them and neither has Tom. Nor do we plan to." Garrett didn't want it getting around. "But it's public record. So they might find out on their own. Or someone in HR might mention it and get tongues wagging. People gossip, even if they've been warned not to."

They stopped in the breezeway of the barn, and Garrett rolled up his shirtsleeves. He'd left his jacket back at his office, but he was still wearing his tie. He had a huge collection of them. He kept them in his closet, organized by color, the same as his suits.

Meagan's skirt was flowing softly around her ankles. Everything about her looked soft and touchable. Not that he ever intended to touch her.

She turned to pat the neck of a big bay gelding poking his head over his stall.

"That's Ho-Dad," Garrett told her.

She smiled. "That's an interesting name for a horse."

"It's an old surf term. It refers to anyone who pesters them when they're on their boards, and Ho-Dad likes surfers, sometimes a little too much. He would probably go surfing himself, if he could."

"Oh, that's cute." Her smile widened. "Can't you just see him out there?"

"In a wet suit? That wouldn't be a pretty sight." Garrett just wished that Meagan wasn't so damned pretty. He didn't need the distraction.

She gave the bay another affectionate pat, and he

noticed how gently she handled the animal. Ho-Dad was enthralled with her already.

"Do you like to ride?" Garrett asked.

"Surfboards?" She laughed a little. Ho-Dad was craning his neck to get closer to her. "Oh, you mean horses? I haven't ridden since I was a kid. Ivy loves being in the saddle, though. Tanner puts her up on his horses with him. It's been good for me to see her enjoying it so much. It was tough for me when I was little."

"What was? Being around horses?" He was curious, far more than he should be. But he still wanted to know exactly what she meant.

She turned away from Ho-Dad, giving Garrett her full attention. "Yes, being around horses became difficult, especially after my baby sister died and my parents got divorced."

"You had a sister?" As far as he knew, his mom hadn't uncovered that bit of information. If she had, she would've mentioned it to him, particularly with how determined she was in this whole forgive-Meagan affair.

She took an audible breath. "It was a terrible time for my family. Mom fell apart, and Dad got even meaner." She glanced at the gelding. "Dad never appreciated horses the way Mom did. In fact, he hated that she and us kids shared the interest. So after the divorce, I took less of an interest in horses, hoping that Dad would be nicer to me. But it didn't make a difference. On occasion I still rode with Mom, just so she didn't feel so neglected. Then, as time went on, I stopped riding altogether because Dad was still trashing us for it."

Garrett had never really thought about the kind of

childhood Meagan might've had. But it wasn't his concern. Still, it bothered him that her dad seemed like such a prick. "Your old man sounds like a piece of work."

"I never should've tried to be a daddy's girl. Not after how he treated my mother."

Garrett debated whether to tell her that his mom and her mom had been loosely connected, that they'd actually belonged to the same Native American women's group when they were younger, even if they'd barely known each other.

No, he thought. He wasn't going to say anything. His mom was already making too big of a deal out of it, and he didn't want Meagan blowing it out of proportion, too.

She cleared her throat. "None of us have anything to do with Dad anymore. Not me or my brothers. I'm not even sure if he knows that I went to prison or that I have a daughter. But he probably wouldn't care, anyway."

"You should start riding again and stick with it this time."

"That's what Tanner said. But he's biased, especially with how much Ivy loves it."

"I keep my horses here. They're on the other side of the barn. I ride nearly every day, so you'll be seeing me around, sometimes in the mornings, other times in the afternoons, depending on my schedule. You can ride here, too, if you want to take it up again. That's a perk that comes with working at the stables. You can use any of the horses that belong to the hotel."

"Thank you. I'll think about it." She smiled at Ho-Dad. He was pestering her to pet him again.

After the tour ended, Garrett and Meagan went back outside, with the grass beneath their feet and the sun shining through the trees.

She glanced around. "It's so pretty here." She looked higher up the hill. "Oh, wow. There's a house up there, all by itself."

Well, hell, Garrett thought. He couldn't very well leave his home out of this. She would find out sooner or later that he resided on the property. "That's where I live. I had it custom-built."

She glanced at him and then back up the hill. "I should have guessed it was yours. It's like a castle that overlooks your kingdom."

He downplayed her words. He didn't like to think of himself that way. "It's just a beach house."

"Well, it looks spectacular, even from here."

Garrett didn't thank her for the compliment. Someday he hoped to have a wife and kids to live there with him. Only he'd yet to find someone who loved him for himself and not his money.

But that was the last thing he wanted to think about, especially while he was in the presence of the beautiful young woman who'd ripped him off. He wasn't going to let her sad story sway him, either. So she'd had a troubled childhood. So had he, but he hadn't become a criminal. Or an ex-con or whatever the hell she was now.

He took her back to the hotel, and they parted ways, with Garrett doing his damnedest to forget about her.

But when he returned to his office, she was still on his mind, burning a fiery hole right through it.

Two

What a day, Meagan thought. But she'd gotten through it. She'd seen Garrett and secured her new job. Still, she was feeling the aftereffects of having been in his company.

And now she needed to go home and decompress. These days, she lived in a guesthouse on Tanner's property, a far cry—thank goodness—from the correctional institution.

She climbed into her car and pulled out of the parking lot. Once she got on the main road, the traffic was heavy, the sights and sounds quick and noisy. Meagan had grown up in LA, but, since she'd gotten out of prison, she felt like a tourist, gawking at the city that surrounded her. Being free was a strange and wondrous feeling. But it was confusing, too. Everything felt different, somehow.

When she arrived at her destination, she parked in front of the main house, a bungalow built in the 1930s, where her brother and Candy resided. With its stucco exterior, brick chimney and stone walkway, it had tons of curb appeal.

Meagan's place, a guesthouse in the back, was just as charming. She even had her own little courtyard that included a patch of grass, a smattering of flowers and a fountain with a naked putto, a Cupid of sorts, who appeared to be peeing in the water. Most people would call it a cherub, but she knew the difference. Cherubs were angels, hailing from heaven, and putti were mythical beings who misbehaved. In that respect, Meagan could relate.

She noticed that Candy's car was missing from the driveway, which meant she was still out and about. She'd taken Ivy grocery shopping with her this afternoon. Tanner was at work and wouldn't be home until later.

For now, Meagan was all alone. She took the side entrance to her house and opened the gate.

She unlocked the front door, went inside and placed her purse on the kitchen table. Next she wandered into Ivy's room. It was fully furnished and decorated in a fairy-tale theme, but Ivy wasn't occupying it yet. Although Ivy had gotten to know Meagan from the prison visits, she'd thrown a panicked fit when they'd tried to move her in with Meagan. Bedtime was the worst. Her daughter absolutely refused to sleep there. So, for the time being, Ivy was still living with Tanner and Candy.

It made Meagan feel like a failure as a mother. But she needed to be patient and give her child time to adjust. It had only been a week.

Meagan went into her own room and heaved a sigh. She sat on the edge of the bed and pulled off her boots.

Barefoot, she returned to the kitchen and checked the microwave clock. To keep herself busy, she brewed a cup of herbal tea and sat in the courtyard. The water from the fountain flowed from tier to tier, making rainlike sounds.

After a short while, she heard a car pull into the driveway. Meagan hopped up and headed over to it.

Candy was just getting out of the driver's side, looking as gorgeous as ever. She was a long, leggy brunette, a former beauty queen and model who'd become a yoga teacher. She and Tanner used to date when they were teenagers. At the time Meagan was only eight, but she'd adored Candy, impressed that her brother was seeing someone so sweet and pretty.

Then, after their baby sister died and their parents started going through the divorce, Tanner couldn't handle having a girlfriend anymore, so he'd broken up with Candy.

Now all these years later, they were back together and engaged to be married. Who knew it would turn out this way? Meagan certainly hadn't seen it coming, especially the part where she ended up in prison while the couple helped raise her child.

Candy walked around to the passenger's side of the

vehicle and removed Ivy from the safety seat. Meagan had one in the backseat of her car, too. Tanner had bought two of them, so they didn't have to switch the same one out all the time.

Ivy was dressed in a bright red romper with her silky brown hair fastened into fancy pigtails sitting high atop her head, twisted and parted in clever ways. Meagan didn't have a clue how to fix her baby's hair like that. It was all Candy's doing.

Ivy glanced over and grinned, waving at Meagan. She wanted to melt on the spot. She waved back, excited by the acknowledgment. Her daughter was the most precious person on earth.

Candy turned and saw Meagan, and they exchanged a smile. Then Candy asked, "How'd the job meeting go?"

"Good. I'll fill you in later, when we're able to sit and talk." Meagan came forward and reached for Ivy. "I can take her now."

"Sure." Candy passed the toddler off. "I'll get the groceries."

"I can help with those, too." Meagan balanced her daughter on her hip, took one of the bags and headed for the back door of the main house.

Once they were inside, she set Ivy down and Candy's dog, a yellow Labrador named Yogi, came into the room.

"Yoey!" Ivy raced toward her canine friend. "See, Mommy? Yoey?"

"Yes, sweetheart, I see her." She loved hearing her daughter mispronounce the dog's name, but she loved hearing her say "Mommy" even more. Ivy had been taught from the beginning who Meagan was. She was too young to grasp it completely, but she liked looking at pictures of animals with their offspring. She knew there were all types of mommies. And daddies, too. That much, she understood.

"Where Tanny?" Ivy asked, using the name she'd learned for Tanner. For Candy, she used Canny.

"Your uncle is at work," Meagan replied.

"Horsey," the child confirmed.

Meagan nodded. "Yes, he works with horses." Tanner owned a riding academy and stables near Griffith Park. He also leased horses to the movie industry. He rode Western and English styles, and Ivy was fascinated with his job.

"I work with horses now, too," Meagan said.

Ivy cocked her head. "Mommy horsey?"

"I'll be taking care of them." At the resort owned by one of the men she'd embezzled from, she thought. But that wasn't something she could tell her daughter. Ivy didn't know that the place where she used to visit Meagan was a prison, and even if she did, it wouldn't have meant anything to her. Someday it would, though. Once Ivy got older, it would be a discussion they were destined to have.

After the groceries were put away, Candy gave Ivy a sippy cup with milk in it, and the child sat on the floor with Yogi, drinking her beverage and pretending to do yoga. Or maybe she was actually doing it for real, to the best of her ability. The dog got into some poses with her.

Besides regular yoga, Candy also taught doga, yoga

for dogs, where the animals exercised with their owners, and Yogi knew her stuff.

Meagan watched her daughter, smiling as Ivy concentrated on her task. She was proud of her little girl but intimidated by how strong Candy's influence was on her. Ivy mirrored the other woman's mannerisms, not Meagan's.

Then again, did she really want Ivy to emulate her? Meagan was still working on becoming the kind of person who would make her daughter proud, and Candy was already an elegant role model. Even as casually as she was dressed, in leggings and an oversized T-shirt, she exhibited grace and style. As a child, Meagan had wanted to grow up to be just like her. Boy, had she missed the mark on that one.

Candy removed a pitcher of lemonade from the fridge. "Want some?"

Meagan nodded. "Sure. Thanks." There was a lemon tree on the property, so it was fresh-squeezed juice.

Candy poured two frosty glasses. Meagan accepted hers, and they sat in the living room, where Ivy and Yogi played.

"You can fill me in now," Candy said.

"Yes, of course. It turned out fine, but I was super nervous seeing Garrett again. He admitted that it wasn't his idea to hire me. His mother convinced him to give me a chance."

"Really?" Candy angled her head. "She must be a nice lady."

"I've never met her. I got a glimpse of her at the sentencing, though. He said that she felt bad for me then, and me having a baby while I was in prison was part of it, too. I guess that affected her somehow. I asked Garrett if I could send her a thank-you card, but he's going to relay the message instead."

"What about the other men? Did you see them?"

"His foster brothers? No. They weren't at this meeting. They don't own the hotel with him. They have their own businesses. One of them is a real estate mogul, and the other one is an internet entrepreneur."

"What type of person is Garrett?"

Meagan drew a breath. "He's…" She couldn't think of the right adjectives to describe him, not without her heart going a little haywire. She'd never told anyone that she used to have feelings for him. Finally she settled on, "He used to be really kind to me."

Candy frowned. "He isn't being kind to you now?"

"He was proper and professional. A bit cautious, I suppose. But he used to go out of his way to treat me like a friend."

"That's confusing."

"What do you mean?"

"Why, of all people, did you embezzle from a man who was good to you? Not that you should steal from anyone, but to choose him? I don't get it."

"I took the money before I met him."

"And afterward?"

"I didn't take any more money, but it was already too late by then. He was really nice to me until he found out what a traitor I was. He even gave me a daisy." She explained how she'd first met him, reciting the details. She left out the part about being attracted to Garrett, though. She didn't think it was wise to mention that. Besides, she didn't want anyone figuring out that she was still having those types of feelings for him. Nonetheless, she admitted how important the daisy had been to her. "I kept the flower for a while. I wrapped it in plastic and tucked it away in my drawer. Neil didn't pay attention to stuff like that. But I finally got rid of it, because every time I looked at it, it made me feel worse about what I'd done."

Candy had a sympathetic expression. "Have I ever told you about the language of flowers?"

Meagan shook her head. "Not that I recall."

"It's called floriography, and it's a method that was used in the Victorian era when people would exchange flowers in lieu of written greetings. I became really fascinated with it, and I taught your brother about it, too. Each flower has a meaning, so you can give someone a single bloom or an entire bouquet to express a certain sentiment or have conversations. I studied a book about it."

"That does sound fascinating." Curious, Meagan asked, "Do you know what daisies mean?"

"Yes, but it depends on what kind they are. English daisies are the most recognizable. They're sometimes called common daisies. But there are other kinds, too."

"I don't know what type it was, except that it was bigger than the usual ones."

"Here." Candy reached for an iPad sitting on a nearby table and gave the device to Meagan. "See if you can find it."

She did an internet search, scrolling through the different varieties until she found the right kind. She noticed how bright and pretty the flowers were and how many colors they came in. Hers had been yellow with double florets. She turned the screen around. "It was a gerbera, like this."

Candy looked at the picture and said, "Those embody friendship. But they can mean sadness and someone needing protection, too."

"All of that works." The sadness Meagan had been feeling that day, the friendship Garrett had offered, the protection she'd needed from her crazy life with Neil. She doubted that Garrett knew any of this. Still, the fact that he'd given her a flower with those meanings gave her goose bumps.

Candy took back the iPad and set it aside. "Isn't it funny how things like that present themselves?"

"Yes." A strange kind of funny. Now she wished that she hadn't disposed of the daisy. If she'd held onto it, it would have been stored with the rest of her belongings. Tanner had kept Meagan's things for her, along with items that had belonged to their mother.

Feeling far too emotional, she glanced at her daughter. Ivy was still playing with the dog, stretching out on the floor and lifting her stubby little legs in the air.

Candy watched the child, too. Then she said, "Tanner and I are going to set the date for the wedding. As you know, we've been waiting to get married so you could be there, and now that you're home, we figured we should start planning it. I want you to be one of my bridesmaids, and I promise I won't make you wear an ugly dress." The bride-to-be smiled. "We'll choose something that you feel glamorous in."

Meagan hadn't felt glamorous in a very long time. "What about a dress for you? It's going to be your special day. That's the dress that really matters."

"Will you help me shop for it?"

"Yes, of course. I'd love to. And I'm honored that you want me to be in your wedding."

"Ivy and Yogi are going to be in it, too. They're both going to be flower girls. I figured that they could walk down the aisle together, but if Ivy falters and runs ahead, that's okay. Tanner and I want the ceremony to be fun."

Meagan smiled, warmed by the thought. She glanced at her daughter again, overwhelmed by how beautiful she was. "That's sweet, and I'm sure Ivy will love it."

Candy sent her a comforting look. "It won't be long before she gets comfortable staying at your house, Meagan."

"Do you think so?"

"Yes, I'm sure of it. You're an amazing mother, and she's going to need you more and more as time goes on."

"Thank you. That means a lot to me."

"Do you want to stay for dinner tonight?" Candy asked. "Or would you rather go back to your place and unwind?"

"I'd like to stay." Being in a family setting felt good, and Meagan knew how important it was for her to spend as much time with Ivy as possible. "After dinner,

I can bathe Ivy and read her a story and tuck her in." They weren't living together yet, but that didn't mean she couldn't be part of her child's bedtime. "I should probably start doing that every night, so she gets used to me putting her to bed."

"That's a great idea." Candy shifted her gaze, glancing in the direction of the kitchen. "I'll make a chicken-and-rice casserole for you and Tanner and Ivy."

"That sounds good. But what are you going to eat?" Her brother's fiancée was vegetarian.

"I'll whip up a spinach soufflé. Of course you guys can eat that, too."

"Does Ivy like spinach?"

"It's one of her favorites."

"That's good to know." Meagan was just learning how to interact with her daughter on a daily basis and that included becoming accustomed to her food habits. "I can help with the meal. I'm out of practice, but I like to cook."

"Did your mom teach you?"

"Yes." Meagan turned toward the fireplace, where a framed photo of her mother was, amid a grouping of other pictures. "I miss her every day."

Candy sighed. "I had a difficult relationship with my mom when I was growing up, but things are good between us now. She adores Tanner and Ivy. She can't wait for me to have kids of my own, too. Whenever she babysits Ivy, she mentions it."

"I'm glad that Ivy is inspiring her to want grandbabies." Meagan knew that Candy had been pregnant once and had miscarried, but that was years ago, when she was married to someone else—a man who hadn't treated her right.

In that respect, Meagan and Candy were alike. They'd both survived controlling relationships. But now Candy had Tanner, the love of her life and the person she was meant to be with.

If the possibility existed, Meagan hoped that someday she would find someone special, too. But at this stage of her life, she was a single mother and brand-new parolee, taking one step at a time on the road to redemption.

In the evening, when Meagan's brother came home from work, Ivy was thrilled to see him.

The instant he opened the door she dashed over to him, calling his name as she knew it. "Tanny! Tanny!"

He scooped her up and gave her a loud smacking kiss. The child giggled and looped her arms around his neck.

Meagan lingered in the background and watched the exchange. At six-three, Tanner was a striking man, with short black hair and slate-gray eyes. Today he was dressed in Western riding gear. He was a darned fine uncle. He'd earned Ivy's love and respect.

Candy heard the commotion and came around the corner, moving forward to greet her fiancé. He kissed her, as well, only it wasn't as noisy as the playful peck he'd bestowed upon Ivy.

"Hey, sis," Tanner said, when he noticed Meagan standing there. "How'd the job stuff go?"

She stepped forward, keeping her response simple. "Good. I'll be starting on Monday."

He smiled and shifted Ivy in his arms. "You're going to do great."

Putting on a brave front, she returned his smile. But deep inside, her nerves were fluttering, a reminder of how working at Garrett's resort was making her feel. "I'm certainly going to try."

"Meagan is staying for dinner," Candy said. "She helped me cook. We've got casseroles in the oven."

"Cool." Tanner sounded pleased. "We can all hang out together." He put Ivy on her feet, and the child toddled off to dig through a basket of toys that was in the living room.

Tanner disappeared, probably to shower and change, and Candy bustled around, setting the table and filling the water glasses.

"Can I help with anything else?" Meagan asked her.

"No, thanks. I've got it under control. You can just relax."

"Okay. Then I'll stay right here." Meagan sat on the floor next to her daughter, using the extra time to try to keep bonding with her.

Ivy reached into the basket and removed a pink plastic pony that had a long purple mane and a green tail. Clipped onto its back was a polka-dotted saddle.

She gave the toy to Meagan and said, "Pay." It was her way of saying, "Play."

Meagan gently obliged. She walked the pony in a slow circle, and Ivy watched it go round and round.

The two-year-old looked a lot like Meagan, with

her dark hair and naturally tanned complexion. She didn't favor blond, blue-eyed Neil, which was just as well. Meagan hadn't seen him since he'd left her, pregnant and alone. He was still somewhere in the area, she suspected. He thrived on the LA club scene. Meagan had done her fair share of partying when she was with Neil, but all she wanted was stability now.

Ivy extended her hand, asking for her pony. "Mine."

Meagan returned it, and the little girl trotted it high in the air, as if it were climbing a magical hill.

Instantly, Meagan thought about Garrett and his ocean-cliff home. She assumed that he'd never been married or had kids. But she couldn't be sure. She didn't know anything about his personal life. She wondered about him and the types of women he dated. As for herself, Neil had been her first and only lover, but she used to fantasize about Garrett something fierce.

"Is everything okay? You seem preoccupied."

She glanced up and saw Tanner staring at her with a concerned look on his face. He'd just returned to the living room, attired in sweatpants and a T-shirt.

She couldn't tell her brother what she'd been thinking. Her thoughts of Garrett were her own, particularly when they concerned sexy things.

"I'm just getting hungry," she said.

"Then you're in luck." Tanner motioned to the kitchen, where Candy was putting the finishing touches on the salad and taking the casseroles out of the oven.

They sat at the dining room table, and Meagan snapped a bib around Ivy. The toddler was raring to go. She even brought the pony with her, setting it on her high chair tray.

Ivy ate both casseroles, quite happily. Dessert, a creamy chocolate pudding, made her even happier. Meagan kept wiping her daughter's mouth and hands. She cleaned the pony, too. Ivy was making a gleeful mess feeding it, as well.

"I can bring Ivy with me when I go to work," Meagan said to Tanner and Candy. "The resort offers free day care and after-school programs for children of the employees. I'm going to check it out and hopefully get her enrolled by Monday."

"That sounds great," her brother replied. "I think it'll be good for Ivy to be in that type of setting, especially with you being nearby."

"I agree," Candy said. "I think Ivy will enjoy it. She likes playing with other kids. I'll miss having her with me every day, but you need to do what's right for yourself and your daughter."

"Thank you." Meagan was glad that everyone approved of the idea. "I appreciate your support."

"I'd like to meet Garrett sometime." Tanner took a second helping of the chicken-and-rice casserole. "He sounds like a pretty decent guy, offering something like that." He turned toward Meagan. "It was decent of him to hire you, too."

Yes, it was, she thought. Even if it had been his mother's idea, he'd still followed through and given her a job. "He told me that I can ride at the resort any time I want."

"Then you should take him up on it." Tanner spoke

softly. "You know I'd like to see you get back on a horse. You're always welcome to ride at my stables, too."

"I know. It might be easier at the resort, though, since I'll already be there for work. And I like the atmosphere." She'd always loved the sand and surf. When she was a teenager, like a slew of other California girls, she used to go the beach with her friends. "If I'm going to ride again, maybe I should start there."

Her brother encouraged her. "So go for it."

Would she come across Garrett on the trail? Would she pass him along the shore? "I'm considering it." Before her nerves ran away with her, she added, "But I don't want to jump into anything too soon."

"You'll be ready when the time comes."

"I hope so." Especially if it involved seeing Garrett. Already she was anxious about their next encounter and how it would unfold. He'd told her that he spent a lot of time at the stables. So one way or another, she had to get used to seeing him.

Tanner went quiet, returning to his food. Meagan lifted her fork and raised it to her mouth, trying to concentrate on her meal, too. But above all else, she needed to clear her troubled mind.

And stop worrying about Garrett.

Three

Garrett headed toward the child care center at the resort. He promised himself that he was going to keep an eye on Meagan, to see what type of person she truly was, so he decided to be there when she dropped her kid off.

Today was Meagan's first day on the job, and he'd learned from HR that she'd enrolled her daughter in the day care. So why shouldn't he be curious to see her with her child, especially on this very first day?

Besides, it wasn't as if he'd never popped over to the day care before. He actually did it quite often. This was his resort, his place of business, and he was a hands-on CEO. He made a point of checking on every department to make sure that things were running smoothly, to speak to everyone employed there. He knew the day care teachers by name. He liked being around the kids, too. When he was in foster care, some of the younger children used to come to him for comfort and support. Sometimes it was for something as simple as a skinned knee. On occasion, it was far more serious, like bullying. He used to look out for Max, his tech-geek foster brother, when Max had been too small and skinny to fend for himself. Garrett was good at protecting the rights of others. He handled his own rights just fine, too.

He sat on a bench in the atrium where the day care was located and sipped his coffee out of a disposable cup. Every workday morning, he got a medium-bodied roast with a dash of milk from the coffee vendor in the food court in the hotel.

Here we go, he thought. His timing was impeccable. He spotted Meagan entering the atrium and holding her daughter's hand. He couldn't help smiling to himself. Her kid was a cute little tyke, toddling along in a denim outfit and pink cowboy boots. In her free hand, she clutched a heart-shaped purse with cartoon characters on it, swinging it as she moved. She walked with a bounce in her step, a ribbon-wrapped ponytail exploding from the top of her head. Meagan was in denim, too, but she looked far more serene in her Western wear. Her long thick hair was plaited into a single braid that hung down her back, and her boots were a neutral shade of brown. She had a hell of a figure. Her jeans cupped her rear like nobody's business.

She glanced over, and their gazes met across the

open space. Garrett stood and tossed his empty cup into a recycle bin.

He walked over to her, and they faced each other, with sunlight spilling down over them, courtesy of the glass roof above their heads.

"I wanted to be here when you brought your daughter to the day care," he said, being as honest as the moment would allow.

Meagan seemed taken aback. Clearly, she hadn't expected his intrusion to be so deliberate. But she recovered quickly and focused on her child. She said to the little girl, "Ivy, this is Garrett. He gave me my job. The one I told you about before, where I'll be working with horses."

The toddler released her mother's hand. Puckering her tiny face, she stared up at Garrett and made an empty gesture, like an actress playing to an audience. "Where horsies?"

Instantly amused by her, he motioned toward a window. "They're outside in the stables." He got down on one knee, putting himself at her level, and asked, "Do you like horses?"

She nodded vigorously and tugged at the Velcro on her purse. Once she got it open, she removed a toy pony and showed it to him. The purse was given to Meagan to hold on to.

Garrett studied the pony and smiled. It looked like a rainbow had thrown up on it, spewing all sorts of colors. "That's the fanciest mare I've ever seen."

"Horsie mine." She pointed to herself. "Iby."

He smiled again and then exchanged a glance with Meagan.

Her mother said, "She can't quite say her name yet. She mispronounces other things, too. But mostly, she has really good language skills for a child her age. She comprehends well, and she's learning new words every day."

"She's beautiful," he replied. "Aren't you, Ivy?"

Proving how much she loved her pony, the animated toddler held it a few inches from her lips and made a kissy sound. Then she brought it about the same distance from Garrett's lips, so he could air-kiss it, too. He laughed and mimicked the sound she'd made. He was totally smitten with this kid.

She pulled the pony away from him and said, "Horsie eat." She pretended the toy was wolfing something down. "See, Mommy?" She looked back at her mother.

"Yes, I see. And I remember that the pony had dinner with you last night." Meagan turned to Garrett and said, "The pony got a bubble bath afterward, too. She had chocolate pudding on her face."

"That's my kind of horse." He tugged Ivy's ponytail and got to his feet, coming to his full height.

Garrett and Meagan made direct eye contact again. He was doing his damnedest not to be as smitten with the mother as he was with the child. To keep his priorities in check, he reminded himself that this was the woman who'd acted all sweet and innocent, even after she'd ripped him off.

"You're good with kids," she said.

"I've always liked children."

"You don't have any, do you?"

He shook his head. He wasn't about to admit that he wanted a houseful. That wasn't anything she needed to know.

"I didn't think so, but I wasn't sure. I guess it's safe to assume you've never been married, either."

"Yes, that's a safe assumption." He'd been looking for the right mate, but so far he hadn't found her. Sometimes he got burned out believing it would happen. His last relationship had ended badly, with his former lover storming out of his life because he wouldn't invest in a half-baked business venture of hers. "Jake is married now, though, with a baby on the way." He added, "You remember Jake," saying it as a not-so-subtle reminder that she'd stolen from him, too.

"Yes, of course." Meagan looked guilty as charged. "He's one of your foster brothers."

Garrett felt something poke his leg. It was Ivy, jabbing him with the pony as she waved the toy around. He relaxed his posture, not wanting the child to absorb the tension he'd just created between himself and her mom.

He softened his voice. "Jake and his wife are having a girl."

"When is the baby due?"

"I'm not sure of the exact date. It's still a few months away. They're over the moon about it. Jake is excited about being in the delivery room. He wants to cradle his daughter the moment she's born."

"That's nice." Even though Meagan smiled, her eyes were edged with pain. "That's how it should be."

Was she thinking about the way in which she'd given birth to her own child? Garrett didn't know if Ivy had been born at the prison itself or if Meagan had been taken to a hospital. Whichever way it happened, he couldn't fathom it. He was sorry if she'd had a rough time of it, but he couldn't bring himself to say those words out loud. Yet he couldn't stay completely silent, either. He felt compelled to say something, if just to keep the conversation going.

He settled on "Jake was a little freaked out at first. He never expected to get married or have kids. He understood what was at stake, that being a parent is the most important job in the world. But I'm sure you already know that."

"Yes, I do." She reached down and scooped up her daughter, holding her close.

Ivy put her head on her mother's shoulder and grinned at Garrett. Then she dropped her pony and said, "Uh-oh."

Little devil. He could tell that she'd done it on purpose. He picked up the toy and handed it to her. Already she had a way with men. No doubt she'd gotten it from her mother.

The kid made an impish face and dropped it again.

"Ivy," her mom gently scolded.

He retrieved the toy a second time. He just couldn't seem to resist.

"Sorry." Meagan set Ivy on her feet.

"It's okay." He gave the child her pony. She was just too damned clever for her own good. They both were.

"Thank you," Meagan said. She urged her daughter to say it, as well. "Tell Garrett thank you."

Ivy obliged with "Tank you, Garry."

His heart melted, all the way to his toes. "You're welcome." He gazed at Meagan, laughed a little and said, "I guess I'm Garry now."

"She calls my brother Tanny and his fiancée Canny. A friend of theirs has a son who called them that when he was first learning to talk, so they taught Ivy to refer to them that way, too." She smiled. "But you just got your nickname all on your own."

"Like a guy who's been knighted?" He made a sweeping bow. "Well done, Princess Ivy."

The toddler stared up at him, and Meagan said, "Oh, that's so sweet, you calling her that. I named her after a princess in a children's book. I read the book when I was in elementary school, and I always remembered the name."

"It suits her." She was a regal kid, with her pink boots, painted pony and long, spiky eyelashes.

"I better get her to the day care." Meagan took Ivy's hand. "Do you want to go inside with us?"

"Sure. Why not?" He could have made an excuse to dash off, but he'd come here to observe Meagan with her daughter, so he might as well see it through to the end. "I like visiting the center."

It went well, with Ivy's teacher showing her around. The toddler seemed excited until she realized that she was going to be left there, without Meagan. She cried and clung to her mother's leg. Both Meagan and the teacher attempted to reassure her, but she wasn't having it. She kept bawling.

Garrett intervened, asking Ivy if she wanted to play blocks with him. She refused, but he didn't give up. He sat on a carpeted section of the floor with some of the other kids, hoping she would get curious and join the party.

Eventually, her sniffles and tears subsided and she wandered over to him. He handed her one of the blocks, which he'd saved exclusively for her, and her eyes grew big and wide. The block had a picture of a horse on it. A lot of them had images of animals. Some had numbers and letters, too.

Meagan stood off to the side and watched him as if he were some sort of hero. He could have kicked himself for it.

He didn't need her admiring him, or getting close to him, or using her beautiful charms and pulling him under her spell.

Finally, when Ivy was chattering with another little girl and stacking the blocks like an architect, Garrett got up from the floor.

"That was wonderful of you," Meagan said to him. "I never anticipated her crying like that."

"She seems okay now."

"Thanks to you."

He shrugged, making light of it, even if there was heaviness inside him. "It's all in a day's work."

"I hope she's going to be okay for the rest of the day."

"She'll be fine." He almost offered to come back and check on her, but he'd already taken this further than he should have. "You can stop by on your lunch hour to see her. Lots of the other parents do that."

"I definitely will. Thank you for everything, Garrett."

"You don't have to keep thanking me."

"You've just done so much to help, with the job and now with Ivy."

Garrett didn't reply. Her daughter's tears had affected him more than he cared to admit. It reminded him of the younger kids who used to cry in foster care.

Ivy turned and waved at her mother, giving her permission to leave, and he and Meagan walked out of the day care together.

"Oh, my goodness," she said, as soon as they were free of the place. "My first experience with taking my baby to school."

Garrett merely nodded. He could tell she was struggling not to break down, but her eyes had turned teary nonetheless. He considered giving her his handkerchief, the way he'd done when they'd originally met. But he refrained from making the gesture. By now, he was supposed to know better.

While he steeled his thoughts, she dabbed at the corners of her eyes with the tips of her knuckles, as if she were trying to wipe away the evidence of her emotions and look stronger than she felt. Only it wasn't working. She still seemed fragile.

But Meagan's vulnerability wasn't his concern. Nor was he going to be sitting on the floor with a bunch of kids for the rest of the morning. He had grown-up meetings to attend. He was leaving tomorrow on a business trip and had a lot to do before then. "I should go."

She quit fussing with her eyes. "Maybe I'll see you later."

"Yeah," he replied, intending to escape with his indifference intact. "Have a good first day of work."

"Thank you. I'll try."

She was clutching her daughter's cartoon character purse as if the bag contained magic. And maybe in some sort of storybook way it did. He could almost imagine stars and moons and bits of glitter coming from it.

They said a quick goodbye and exited the atrium, going in different directions. But being separated from Meagan didn't stop Garrett from thinking about her. Once again, he couldn't seem to shake her, no matter how hard he tried.

Meagan hadn't seen Garrett since he'd soothed Ivy at the day care, and that was a week ago. Time was moving on already. Today was her second Monday on the job, and she was doing well at work. But she couldn't help wondering why he hadn't come by the stables. She'd expected to catch sight of him at the barn, hanging out with his horses or going for a ride. But he was nowhere to be seen, at least not while Meagan was present.

Was it a coincidence that he hadn't been there? Or was he staying away on purpose, distancing himself from her?

She spoke to the gelding she was grooming. "What do you think, Ho-Dad?"

The horse blew out a breath as if to say she was jumping to conclusions.

She laughed. "You're right. Why would he go out of his way to avoid me? If he wanted to ride, he would come here and saddle up. He's probably just had a heavy schedule."

Ho-Dad bobbed his head, and she decided, a bit foolishly, that he actually understood what she was saying. Still, she wished that Garrett would appear, just so she could get accustomed to being around him. Otherwise, her stomach would keep tying itself up in little knots. Or tangled butterflies, or whatever they were.

The gelding stood there patiently as she continued grooming him. When she was finished, she gave him a carrot, offering it to him from the flat of her hand.

As Ho-Dad chewed and dropped tiny orange bits from his mouth, she heard a man say, "Are you spoiling that surfer boy?"

Meagan's heart pounded like a drumbeat in her chest. She recognized Garrett's voice. She'd wished that he would appear, and now he was here.

Preparing to face him, she turned all the way around. He was standing on the other side of the stall, dressed in jeans, a casual Western shirt and boots. Obviously, he was planning on riding this afternoon.

"Ho-Dad is my favorite," she said, trying to keep herself calm.

Garrett nodded. "I figured he would be."

She struggled to act normally. The horse was

chomping his treat in her ear, and her heart was thumping just as loudly. "Have you been busy?"

"Why do you ask?"

"You haven't been at the barn."

Garrett raised his eyebrows. "You've been keeping tabs on me?"

Meagan nearly winced. She wasn't doing a very good job of seeming normal. "I just noticed that you haven't been here. You told me that you ride nearly every day and that I would see you at barn, but you haven't been around. So I wondered about it."

"I was in Las Vegas at a hospitality convention. I'm leaving again in a few days, so I'll be gone again."

"For how long?"

"Another week. It's for business, too."

"Do you travel a lot for work?"

"Not necessarily. I prefer staying home and running the resort, but sometimes it can't be helped." He shifted his stance. "I'm here now, though, and ready to ride."

Yes, he most definitely was. She was used to cowboys, both of her brothers being that type. But Garrett was altering her perspective. With the sexy goose bumps he was giving her, she was seeing Western men in a far less brotherly way. Or this man, anyway. But she'd always had a hot and dizzying thing for him, so she'd been doomed from the start.

Ho-Dad nudged her shoulder, bugging her for another carrot. Normally she gave him two. Already they'd established a routine.

"Go ahead," Garrett said.

"Go ahead and what?" she asked.

"Give him the other one. I can tell that's the pattern between you."

Either Garrett was highly observant or she and the horse were ridiculously transparent. She removed the second carrot from her pocket and offered it to Ho-Dad, and the gelding took it eagerly.

Meagan stayed inside the stall, even though she didn't need to. She was done with Ho-Dad. But for now, the stall seemed like the safest place to be, acting as a barrier and keeping her from getting too close to Garrett.

He said, "Tom told me you're doing a great job."

Ah, yes, Tom. Her kindly old boss. "I appreciate him saying that."

"He also said that you hardly ever take breaks."

"I take a lunch every day. That's when I go to the day care to see Ivy."

"He was referring to breaks in-between. He thinks you work harder than anyone else here."

"That's not a bad thing, is it?"

"No, of course not. But you're allowed to have a moment to yourself, Meagan."

"I'm used to living by someone else's time clock."

"What do you mean? When you were locked up?"

She nodded. "I was a level-one inmate, the least dangerous type of offender, so I lived in an open dormitory with a low security perimeter. But it was still regimented." She added, "In the beginning when I was pregnant with Ivy, I was considered special needs and was kept in a unit with other pregnant women."

"Where did you give birth?"

"In a hospital. They transported me there from the prison, but I was lucky they didn't put me in waist chains or leg irons or handcuff my hands behind my body. That's been outlawed in California."

"Damn," he said. "Did you get to see Ivy or hold her?"

"Yes, but not for very long. Thankfully, the hospital staff was nice to me. It's not always like that. Some pregnant inmates have had horrendous experiences, with the doctors and nurses being mean or indifferent to them. But I was still really scared. I wasn't allowed to have a birthing coach. Or see my family. By the time Tanner was notified, and he and Candy picked Ivy up from the hospital, I was already gone, back at the prison."

"That sounds terribly lonely."

"It was, but it's my own fault. I'm the one who committed a crime. You know better than anyone what I did."

"Yes, but having a baby shouldn't be like that." He looked like he wanted to touch her, to comfort her in some way, but he gripped the stall door instead. Neither of them spoke again, until he said, "I still want you to take breaks while you're here."

"All right." She didn't want to make waves, even if it was for working too hard. "I'm taking a break right now, talking to you."

"I suppose you are." He swept his gaze over her. "So how are your lunch visits with Ivy? Is she enjoying the day care?"

"Yes, she's settling in beautifully. She's excited to

go to work with me and play with her new friends at school. But she keeps asking me about the horses. She wants to see them."

"Then bring her here and show her around."

"That would be okay?"

"Sure. You can bring her here today, if you want to, after your shift."

"She would love that." Meagan dusted her hands on her jeans, debating whether to tell him how interested her daughter was in him. But for her child's sake, she went ahead and said it. "Ivy hasn't just been asking me about the horses—she's also been asking me about you."

"She has?" He sounded surprised. "What did she say?"

"She's been wondering why you haven't come back to the day care to see her."

"Really?" He squinted, but he smiled a little, too. "I thought about checking up on her, but I didn't think it was my place."

"Are you kidding? She would be thrilled. She keeps asking, 'Where Garry?' Apparently, you made quite an impression with how attentive you were to her. I also think you remind her of Tanner. Your hair is the same color as his, and you have a similar height and build. She's really close to him, so it would stand to reason that she would feel comfortable around you, too."

"If you bring her here after you get off work, I'll probably be here anyway, finishing up my ride, as late in the day as it is now. Then we can all look at the horses together."

"Okay. Sure." Meagan's heart hadn't quit pounding, and now it was really racing up a storm. Doing something "together" with Garrett and Ivy seemed sweetly intimate. Her fantasies about him had begun to progress in ways she'd never expected. "I want Ivy to meet Ho-Dad most of all."

"He certainly likes you." Garrett glanced at the horse and then back at her. "I'm going to go for my ride now. I'll catch you and Ivy later."

"Yes, later." She watched him walk away, much too excited about seeing him again.

Four

When Garrett returned to the barn, Meagan wasn't there. But he figured she was probably picking up her daughter and would arrive soon. He gave his horse to one of the other stable hands and waited out front.

He was flattered that Ivy had been asking about him, but should he really be doing this?

No, he thought, he shouldn't be. But he couldn't ditch Meagan or her kid. That would be cruel to the child. And to Meagan, too.

But he wasn't supposed to give a damn about Meagan. He was only doing this for Ivy, he told himself. She deserved all the breaks she could get.

And Meagan didn't? His mother would argue the point. Even Jake and Max weren't as pissed about the embezzlement as he was. But his foster brothers hadn't wanted to date Meagan, either. They'd barely even known her. It was different for Garrett. She'd tricked him into liking her.

Was she tricking him again? Or was he just overreacting to the past? He honestly didn't know.

Meagan arrived and pulled into the parking lot. While she parked her car, he stood in the dirt, releasing the air in his lungs and gearing up for this little get-together he'd initiated.

Meagan exited the vehicle and removed Ivy from the backseat. As soon as the toddler saw him, she shot him a chubby-cheeked smile. She was wearing the same frilly pink boots he'd seen her in before.

"Garry!" she said, as he moved closer to her.

"Hello, Princess Ivy," he replied.

She extended both arms, and he assumed that she wanted him to pick her up. He looked at Meagan, making sure it was all right with her. She nodded, and just like that, he was holding Ivy, as if he'd been doing it ever since she was an infant.

"See horsies?" she asked him.

"Yes. We're going to see them."

They entered the barn, and Ivy oohed and ahhed over everything. Even horse turds excited this kid. She squirmed a lot, like children her age typically did. Garrett had to keep a secure hold on her. He even danced her around a bit, making her laugh.

As they stopped at Ho-Dad's stall, he wondered what it would be like to get this close to Meagan, to dance with her, too, which was about the worst thought he could've had.

Dancing with Meagan was off the table. Way off the table. No way in hell was he going to put himself in a situation like that. He was supposed to be over his interest in her.

"This is Ho-Dad," she told her daughter. "He's my favorite."

"Him a daddy?" Ivy asked, leaning forward in Garrett's arms to check out the big bay.

"No, that's just his name," Meagan replied.

Ivy made a perplexed face. "Him no daddy?"

"No, sweetheart, he's not. Geldings are boys, but they aren't daddies."

Ivy decided otherwise. "Yes, him is."

Garrett exchanged a glance with Meagan, and they both smiled. Ho-Dad was as low-key as it got, a far cry from the stud Ivy was making him out to be.

"Do you want to pet him?" Garrett asked her.

She nodded, and he explained how to stroke the horse's neck, but she already knew. Her uncle Tanner must have taught her. She was cautious and gentle, which was a valuable lesson. Some horses spooked when you came at them. Ho-Dad, however, loved being touched. You could go right for his nose, and he wouldn't care. He thrived on any kind of affection.

She called the gelding "Daddy" while she petted him.

And suddenly Garrett thought about the man who'd fathered Ivy and what a jerk he was, cutting this precious child out of his life. But he wasn't going to say that to Meagan, at least not in front of Ivy.

Yet somehow that didn't stop him from blurting

out the truth about his own missing father. "I've never met my dad."

Meagan turned to look at him. "You haven't?"

"No. He was a college student at Oklahoma State, which is near the area where my mother is from. They dated for about a year, but when she got pregnant, he didn't want any part of it. He left town soon after that, and she never saw him again."

"Does she know where he went?"

Garrett shook his head. "She didn't try to track him down, but she assumed that he transferred to another school somewhere. It's tough to say where he is now or if he ever got married or has any other kids. But I don't care. I'm not interested in knowing him."

"I don't blame you." Meagan crinkled her forehead. "Do you think your mother loved him or was it more of a casual relationship?"

"I have no idea. She never talked about it, and I never asked."

"My mom loved my dad, far more than she should have. She used to cry about the divorce, even years later, wishing he would come back to her." She paused. "I think her desperation influenced me in the way I took to Neil and all of the crazy stuff I did for him."

Garrett was curious to know more about her relationship with Neil, but he didn't question her about it, not while he was holding the other man's child.

Ivy stopped petting Ho-Dad and put her head on Garrett's shoulder. He adjusted her to a more comfortable position, letting her use him as a pillow.

Meagan watched how gently he handled her daughter and smiled. Garrett felt her admiration all the way to the pit of his stomach.

"Why were you in foster care?" she asked after a pause.

He quietly replied, "My mother was sick when I was a kid, and there were times that she couldn't take care of me." He gave her the condensed version, keeping the painful details to himself. He'd spent a good portion of his childhood worrying that his mom was going to die.

"Oh, I'm sorry. Is she well now?"

"As well as can be expected. She has an autoimmune disease, so sometimes she still suffers from it."

"Does she live with you?"

"No. She lives at the hotel. She likes it there." He frowned. "I shouldn't be telling you all of this about her."

"Why? Because you're concerned I might contact her? I promise that I won't. But did you relay my message to her?"

"Not yet." He had too much else going on. "I'll do it after I get back from this next trip."

"I appreciate that. I really want your mom to know how grateful I am to her for her involvement in all of this."

"Yeah, I know." But "all of this," as she put it, was getting more complicated than he'd bargained for. Already he was sharing details about himself that he hadn't intended to reveal.

He changed the subject to something less personal. "Have you given any more thought to getting back on a horse?"

"I'm still considering it."

"You should ride Ho-Dad. You've already established a rapport with him, and he's a gentle old soul. He'd be a great mount for you, starting over the way you would be."

"That's good to know. Because he would be my first choice, too." She gazed at Ivy nuzzled against Garrett. "She looks content."

He warned himself, for the umpteenth time, that he was getting closer to Meagan and her daughter than he should be. "Yes, she does. But maybe you should take her now." He transferred Ivy into her mother's arms, hoping the separation would help.

But it didn't. When it came time for them to leave, he didn't want them to go.

He walked Meagan back outside. By now, the child was nodding off, her head drooping forward.

"It must be nap time," he said.

Meagan nodded. "She can nap just about anywhere. She's fussier at bedtime. She cries if she's not in her crib at Tanner and Candy's. I live in a cottage in the back, but Ivy hasn't moved in with me yet." When they got to Meagan's car, she double-checked the buckle on the car seat, making sure it was latched. "For now, I'm tucking her in each night at their house, so she gets used to me being the one who reads her a story and puts her to bed."

He glanced at Ivy. Her eyes were completely closed. "She sure is a sweet kid."

"Thank you." Meagan smiled. "And thank you for

spending this time with us. It meant a lot to Ivy, and to me, too."

Damn. This goodbye was drilling a cozy little hole inside his heart. "Be safe on your way home."

"We will."

She got behind the wheel and started the engine. After she drove away, he remained at the stables, immersed in a stream of warmth he didn't want to feel.

Meagan spent Saturday afternoon with Candy at a bridal salon, where Candy was hoping to find a wedding dress. Dana Reeves was there, too. She was a happy-go-lucky blonde, a self-proclaimed "bohemian" with a fresh and fun nature. She was also Candy's best friend and the matron of honor.

The date had been set for three months from now, and there was a lot of preparation in the works. The ceremony would be held at Tanner's stables and riding academy, where there was plenty of outdoor space, as well as a banquet hall that had been built for special events.

Meagan and Dana were waiting for Candy to come out of the fitting room. A salesgirl—or consultant, as they were called here—had gone in there with her and was helping with all of the buttons, lace and bows. Candy had already tried on a batch of gowns and none of them had been quite right, so she was trying on another round of dresses for them to view.

"I've never been to a bridal shop or participated in a wedding before," Meagan said.

"Really?" Dana smiled, her blues eyes sparkling.

"How exciting this must be for you." She shifted in her seat. "Did you know that Candy hosted my wedding?"

"No, I didn't." All Meagan knew was that Dana's husband's name was Eric, and they had a young son they called Jude. He was the kid who'd come up with the Canny and Tanny nicknames that Ivy used. "Was it at the house where she and Tanner are now?"

"Yes, in the garden. But it was before she sold the place to him or they started seeing each other again."

Meagan nodded. Tanner had purchased the property from Candy when he was looking for a house with a guesthouse that would accommodate Meagan after she got out of prison. At the time, Candy had been going through a financial struggle and couldn't afford to keep her home.

Dana smiled once again. "I like thinking of you being in the guesthouse. I used to live there, too. I was Candy's tenant way back when. That's how we met."

"I wasn't aware of that." Meagan hadn't considered how Candy and her BFF had gotten to know each other.

"For me it was a magical place, like an enchanted cottage."

"It does have that vibe." Meagan couldn't deny that she felt that way about it, too. She just wished that Ivy was staying there with her. But in time she would be. Then it would be even more enchanted.

"I brought Eric there on our first date." Dana all but swooned. Beneath the store's bright lights, her pale yellow hair was shining. Her fair skin seemed almost iridescent, too. "It was one of the most romantic nights of my life." Dana leaned closer. "Maybe some of it will rub off on you."

Meagan felt the other woman's shoulder brush hers, as if the "rubbing off" was happening already.

Naturally, her mind drifted to Garrett. Every time she thought about the paternal way in which he held Ivy, she could barely breathe. Exchanging glances with him left her breathless, too. She used to wonder if he was as attracted to her as she was to him, but now she was pretty darned sure that he was.

Maybe it was better that he was going to be gone this coming week. Maybe she could use that time to start riding again and try to free her mind. Of course, once he returned, she would probably get all fluttery over him again.

Dana watched her for a second and then said, "I hope Candy finds just the right dress."

Grateful for the change of topic, Meagan asked, "Did you wear a traditional gown at your wedding?"

"No. But Candy helped me shop for it. We went to vintage stores because I wanted to keep the cost down. And I love those old styles. It was a cocktail dress from the 1970s, with multicolored jewels on it in the shapes of daisies."

Meagan's heart bumped in her chest. "Daisies?"

"Yes. I got these really cool hairpins to match, too. And then Eric surprised me with an Edwardian daisy-cluster ring." Dana held out her left hand. "See? It goes with my wedding band. He had them soldered together."

"It's beautiful." The ring consisted of a series of

natural-cut diamonds forming a single daisy, reminding Meagan of the flower Garrett had given her. Only the ring looked to be an English daisy, whereas the variety she'd received had been a gerbera. "Candy taught me a little bit about the floriography she's been studying."

"It's interesting, isn't it?"

"Yes." Meagan had discovered that Candy was going to use white roses in her wedding. They represented unity and love.

A few minutes later, the bride-to-be emerged from the fitting room. She stepped up onto the platform to show them the silk dress she was wearing, and Meagan and Dana gasped in unison.

The strapless gown had a mermaid silhouette, with a sweetheart neckline, a keyhole design in back and lace embellishments. The design was stunning on Candy: classic elegance with a court train.

"I love it," Dana said.

"Me, too," Meagan chimed in.

"So do I." Candy swirled, making the hem swish. "I just found my dress."

"You most definitely did." Dana got teary eyed.

Meagan's eyes misted, too. "You're going to be the most gorgeous bride ever. My brother is going to love how you look in it."

"Thank you." Candy gazed at herself in the three-way mirror. "It needs a nip here and tuck there." She glanced at the consultant, who stood nearby, ready to help. "But you'll take care of that."

"Yes, we most certainly will" came the woman's

reply. "And you can order a matching jacket for it, if you want."

"I should probably do that, with it being a winter wedding." Candy turned back around. "I'm so excited."

"As you should be." Dana approached the platform, gazing up at her friend. "Now all you need is something borrowed and something blue."

Candy seemed to think about it for moment. Then she replied, "I can slip a blue rose into my bouquet. All white roses, except for one blue one."

"I've never seen a blue rose," Meagan said. Not that she was an authority on what colors they came in. She was just learning about flowers only now.

"They're not found in nature," Candy told her. "Horticulturists have been working on it for years, but the results always look sort of purplish, rather than a deep, rich blue. So if I want that type of pigment, it'll have to be dyed."

Curious to know more, Meagan asked, "Do they have a floriography meaning?"

"Not in the Victorian dictionary, but they've acquired one since then. The unattainable dream." Candy swayed in her dress. "Only I'll be realizing my dream by marrying Tanner, so adding a blue rose to my bouquet will signify something truly extraordinary for us."

"That's a wonderful sentiment." Meagan loved the idea. Everything about it just seemed so right. But it was especially exciting when Candy decided that the rest of the women in the bridal party should also carry one. It made Meagan feel as if someday something extraordinary could happen to her, too.

* * *

When Garrett returned from his trip, he stopped by his mom's penthouse to see her. She lived on the top floor of the hotel, with a view of the ocean. Her place was cluttered with knickknacks: scented candles, polished stones, glass figurines in the forms of fantasy creatures. Everywhere he looked, he saw dragons, fairies and unicorns. She practiced the old Cheyenne ways, but she dabbled in metaphysical-type stuff, too. In that regard, she was a bit of an enigma. Then again, so was he. His beliefs were as abstract as hers, but that was how she'd raised him.

"Hey, Mom." He sat beside her on her wine-colored sofa and studied her. She was fifty years old, with graying black hair, warm brown eyes and sculpted cheekbones. Even as pretty as she was, she had deep lines etched in her face. Her ill health had taken its toll, beating her up over the years. "How are you?"

"I'm fine." She smiled softly. "I missed you while you were gone. You've been so busy lately."

He shrugged. "I'm always busy."

"I know but more than usual."

"I've had a lot going on, but I'm home now and settling back into things."

"Things?"

"Running the resort."

"Did Meagan start working at the stables yet?"

"Yes." His stomach tightened. Even while he was out of town, he'd thought about Meagan, consumed with the tension of becoming reacquainted with her. "This will be her third week."

"Three weeks?" Mom's eyes went wide. "Why didn't you tell me she's been there that long?"

"Because you're just asking me about it now." When his mother shot him a calculated look, he added, "And I've been gone for most of that time."

She nodded, accepting his explanation. But he knew the conversation wasn't over. She wouldn't let it go that easily. Besides, if he was too closemouthed, that might set off alarm bells, and the last thing he wanted was for his mother to figure out how Meagan was making him feel.

He said, "Tom said that she's doing a good job. That she works hard. I met her kid, too. She's a sweet little girl. Oh, and Meagan asked me to thank you for convincing me to hire her."

"You told her the truth about why you hired her?"

"I wasn't going to lie and pretend that it was my idea."

"Are you being nice to her?"

Because he didn't know how else to respond, he said, "I'm treating her like any other employee."

"You better be."

"I just told you I am." Except that none of his other employees left him reeling the way she did. He didn't go to bed at night thinking about any of them. He was still imagining how it would feel to get close enough to Meagan to dance with her, to sweep her into his arms and spin her around.

"Did you tell her about the day care? Did she enroll her daughter?"

"Yes, she's bringing her there." He thought about

how horribly Ivy had cried on that very first day. He hoped that he never had to see her bawl that way again. "I helped her get the child settled in."

"Really?" Mom seemed impressed. She even sat a little straighter, smoothing her broom-style skirt over her long, rickety legs. "I guess you really are being nice."

His heart went thick, heavy with emotion. "I'm not an ogre." He cared about being a good person.

"I know." She patted his knee. "But you were just so angry about the embezzlement. I'd never seen you that ticked off before. Carrying around all of that negativity isn't good for you."

"It isn't good getting duped by someone, either. There's no guarantee that she can be trusted."

"Has she given you a reason to believe that she would ever commit another crime?"

"No." But what the hell did he know, except that she was driving him mad? "She appears to be a nice girl, always saying how sorry she is. But I thought she was nice before I discovered that she ripped us off."

"Just keep giving her a chance, okay?"

"I'm trying to give her the benefit of the doubt." And it wasn't just that. As deeply as Meagan was burrowing into his brain, he could barely concentrate on anything else.

"Were you becoming friends with her before? Is that why you got so angry about what she did?"

"Yes, that's pretty much it." That and how insanely attracted to her he'd been. And still was, he amended. But that was a secret he was keeping to himself.

His mother peppered him with questions. "Do you think you'll ever become friends with her again?"

"I don't know. It's too early to know how it'll pan out." Nor did he want to think too deeply about that right now.

"Did you tell her that I once knew her mother?"

He squared his shoulders. "No."

"Why not?"

Bloody hell. He was more than ready for this discussion to end. But Mom was gazing at him in that persistent way of hers, waiting for him to respond. "Because I don't want her bugging you about it."

She rolled her eyes at his choice of words. "She wouldn't be bugging me. I would be more than happy to discuss it with her."

"Yeah, well, I told her not to contact you, and she promised that she wouldn't. You already got involved in this more than you should have."

"I got involved because I knew it was the right thing to do, and at some point I'd like to meet her."

"I'd rather that you didn't."

Mom set her jaw. "You can't stop me, Garrett. Sooner or later, I intend to meet her."

Rather than incite an argument, he said, "All right, we'll see how it goes. But for now, just let me handle it."

He wanted to be in control of the situation, to deal with Meagan in his own way, however he could.

Five

After Garrett left his mom's, he went for a ride, needing to unwind and enjoy the elements. The weather was refreshing, with a light breeze and the scent of the surf and sand in the air. The beach was relatively quiet, he noticed, but it usually was this time of year. Nonetheless, the resort still got plenty of business. His place was an LA hotspot, catering to a variety of clientele.

He hadn't seen Meagan at the barn when he'd saddled his horse and figured she was already gone for the day. He'd more or less planned it that way. He wanted this to be a stress-free ride, without the tension that being around her caused.

Hot and sexy tension, he thought. No, he didn't need that today.

He took his horse along the shore, and everything

went splendidly until he spotted another lone figure coming toward him, also on horseback.

From this distance, he couldn't be sure who it was. But his radar went off, anyway. Something told him it was Meagan. A feeling. A gut instinct.

As the horse and rider came closer, his intuition was confirmed. It was Meagan, and she was riding Ho-Dad.

When they were close enough to look into each other's eyes, they both reined their mounts to a stop. While he battled the feelings he'd been trying to avoid, tiny tendrils of hair escaped from her braid and fluttered around her face.

"You did it," he said, congratulating her. "You're riding again."

She nodded and smiled. "Yes, and it's been wonderful, more therapeutic than I imagined. I started last week."

During the time he was gone? Had she done that deliberately or had it just happened that way? He wasn't going to ask, not at the risk of making it sound more important than it was. Instead he inquired, "How often have you been out?"

"Nearly every day. Ivy is doing so well at the day care I either bring her early or keep her a little later, so I can ride."

"You and Ho-Dad make a good pair."

"You said that we would."

"And I was right." But damn if she wasn't killing him. When she leaned forward, patting the side of the gelding's neck, her button-down blouse gaped a bit in front, exposing a hint of flesh. "Have you gone into the hills yet?"

She shook her head and settled back into her seat. "I've been sticking to the beach. But I've been tempted to make my way up there."

"You should."

"Which trails do you think are the best?"

He motioned to the area just east of the stables. "If I were you, I'd go that way. It's nice and wide, and there's a plateau at the top, where you can picnic or relax or whatever."

"That's in the direction where you live," she replied, pointing out the obvious.

"Yes, but the road leading to my house is private." He tried not to fixate on her mouth. But he got lost in his own stupidity and wondered what kissing her would be like. Her lips looked soft and shiny, like she was wearing a glossy balm on them. Maybe one of those flavored kinds? "No one has access to that part of the property except me."

"I can see why you chose such an isolated area to build your house, with how active your work life is. You're around people at the hotel all the time."

And now he was on the beach with her, a woman he still didn't know if he could trust. "Are you going to head into the hills today?"

"I don't think I have time. I've already been out for a while, so I'll need to get back to the day care and pick up Ivy soon. Maybe I'll go into the hills tomorrow."

He took a moment to think, to get his mental bearings. Would it be a mistake to offer to accompany her?

Or would it be a good way to get to know her better, to figure out who and what she really was?

He decided to make the offer. He had a right to gauge her sincerity, to pick her brain and see where it led.

"If you want some company, I can be your guide," he said.

She hesitated. Then she asked, "You'd do that for me?"

"Sure," he replied, even though he would be doing it for himself. "We can try to be friends, can't we?" *Or at least have the illusion of friendship*, he thought. For now, he didn't know if forming a genuine truce with her was possible.

Her gaze locked gently onto his. "That would be nice. And different from before, with the way I deceived you when you thought we were becoming friends."

He almost felt guilty for deceiving her this time. But he couldn't just jump into trusting her that easily. Nor could he keep fantasizing about kissing her. Whatever conclusions he came to about her character, the rest of it would be strictly platonic.

"What time of the day would be better for you?" he asked. "Morning or afternoon? I'm open to either."

"Let's do morning. I can meet you at the stables a few hours before I start my shift."

"Sounds good. I'll see you then."

"Thank you, Garrett. I'm looking forward to it." She said goodbye and headed back to the barn.

He kept going, riding along the shore, hoping that building a "friendship" with her wasn't going to be a mistake.

Meagan rode with Garrett the next morning, trying to keep from staring at him. He was riding the same horse she'd seen him on yesterday—a muscular gelding, shiny and black. Both horse and man looked strong and handsome.

The air was crisp at this early hour. Garrett was dressed for the weather, with a rugged jacket over his shirt. Meagan had a jacket on, too. Later, it was supposed to warm up.

He took her on the trails that led toward the plateau he'd told her about. They barely talked on the way. Mostly, they just absorbed the scenery—dirt and brush and rocks, along with flowering weeds shooting up through the ground, creating colorful patches of prettiness.

When they reached the plateau, she gasped at the sight. It was an open field, as beautiful as could as be, with scattered grass and plush ground cover in various shades of green. There were trees, too, branching their way to the sky.

"This is incredible," she said. It was like being in a whole other dimension. In one direction, she could see the ocean far below. In the other, she sighted the resort and the city that surrounded it.

He watched her as she took it all in. "Do you want to dismount? Maybe kick back awhile?"

Meagan nodded. She could stay here forever.

They tied up their horses, and he spread a gray-and-maroon blanket on the ground.

She stood off to the side. "You came prepared."

He shrugged, smiled. "What kind of Cheyenne would I be if I didn't keep a blanket handy?"

"Well, I'm glad we're here, getting to do this." She was overwhelmed with him actually wanting to attempt a friendship with her. Between the beauty of the land and being here with him, she felt like she was floating. It was odd, though, how tangible he suddenly seemed. Even the tiny crow's-feet around his eyes jumped out at her. She suspected they were mostly frown lines, even if they appeared when he smiled, too.

They sat across from each other. They both had water bottles they'd packed. She sipped from hers while he took a larger swig from his.

"I never asked you about your trip," she said. "How did it go?"

"It was productive. I had meetings and luncheons and those sorts of things. It's good to be back, though. What did you do while I was gone, besides work? And ride," he added.

"That was about it." She paused to refine her answer. "I also went shopping with Candy and a friend of hers for Candy's wedding dress. She and my brother set the date for three months from now."

"Three months?" Garrett shook his head. "What's the hurry?"

"They're just anxious to make it official. They've been engaged for two years, but they've been waiting for me, so I could be part of it."

"We have lots of nuptials here, at the resort, with on-site event planners who handle the details. Typically, it takes about fourteen months to plan a wedding. The quickest one we've ever done was for Jake. He was in a bit of a rush because of the baby, but it turned out beautifully. They exchanged their vows on the beach."

Meagan glanced toward the ocean, picturing the bride's veil billowing in the wind. "Who did he marry?"

"Her name is Carol. She's his personal assistant, so he's always been really reliant on her. He just never expected to fall in love with her and certainly not to the degree he did."

"I heard that Jake was a party boy. That he was really wild and that he dated models and actresses and heiresses. Or that's what people at the accounting firm used to say about him."

"That's true. He played around a lot. But he's different now that he's with Carol. He's a great husband, and he's going to be a wonderful father, too."

"Were you his best man?" In her mind's eye, Meagan saw him in a sleek black tux, his hair combed straight back, his posture tall and straight.

"Yes, me and Max. We both stood up for him."

"People at the firm used to gossip about you and Max, too."

"Oh, yeah?" Garrett stretched out his legs. "What sorts of things did they say?"

"Max was painted as a bit of a mystery. Supersmart but sort of offbeat and reclusive, too. He was rumored to have lots of lovers, except that he didn't show them off the way Jake did. I think that was part of why people thought he was a mystery, with him keeping his women to himself."

"And me?" Garrett asked, his gaze boring into hers. "How was I portrayed?"

She toyed with a corner of the blanket, unnerved by the deep, dark way he was looking at her. "They said that you were the toughest of the three, hard-edged and difficult to get to know." She twisted the material. "I envisioned you as being really ruthless. But you weren't like that when I met you."

"I do have a hard-edged side." His voice went rough. "But it's not as bad as they made it sound. Or at least I don't think it is."

"Maybe you just confuse people."

"Do I confuse you?"

"Sometimes." She was feeling that way right now. But it was different for her, given their history.

Garrett drank more of his water. Meagan was getting thirsty again, too. Or maybe she was feeling the need to do what he did. Either way, she took a sip.

"So what was the rest of the gossip about me?" he asked.

She put down her bottle. "What do you mean?"

"Did they mention my love life? Did they have an opinion on that?"

Her pulse jumped at the line of questioning. "As far as I know, it was never discussed." But she wished it had been. Oh, how she wished. "I'm not sure why no one ever brought it up."

"I don't know whether to be relieved or offended by their lack of interest."

"I think it just makes you even more of a mystery than Max." She quickly added, "Not that it's anyone's business who either of you date." Even if she longed for answers, even if she hoped that he would reveal more about who he was.

But he didn't say a word, leaving her to her own devices.

"I started seeing Neil when I was nineteen," she said, giving him a bit of insight into who she was beyond what he already knew. "I had other boyfriends before him, but he was my first serious relationship. The only man I've ever been with."

"You mean slept with?"

She nodded, and, suddenly, there was a shift in the air between them. Garrett started roaming his gaze over her, checking her out from the top of her head to the tips of her plain and simple boots.

He was making her much too warm. She even removed her jacket. He took off his, too. Then they just sat there, steeped in the awareness of each other.

Until he asked, "What was it about Neil that you were attracted to?"

That was a loaded question, she thought. But she answered it the best she could. "I was young and insecure, and he was bold and adventurous. In some ways, he reminded me of my dad. That sounds so clichéd, but that's how he affected me. Only, unlike my father, Neil treated me like I mattered. Or he did in the beginning, anyway. Later, he expected more out of me than was right." She expelled a shaky breath. "Like asking me to commit a crime."

Garrett kept his gaze trained on her. But he didn't comment. He just listened.

"I'm not saying that what I did is Neil's fault. I should have had the common sense to say no."

"Then why didn't you?"

"I thought that taking the money would make me more exciting in Neil's eyes. And that he would love me." She hated how pathetic she'd been back then, a girl whose every action was born of desperation. "He never actually told me that he loved me, and it was the one thing I kept waiting to hear."

"Did he say it after you took the money?"

Shame coiled in her heart. "Yes, he did. But it felt hollow, especially after I met you. Before then, you and your foster brothers were just some rich guys who weren't going to miss the money. Or that's what I kept telling myself. But when you stopped to comfort me that day, all the remorse I'd been fighting came rushing to the surface." She was feeling it now, too. "I even kept the flower you gave me. But I was too guilty to keep it forever."

"I wasn't expecting you to keep it, let alone forever." His tone sounded a little raw.

Her words went raw, too. "I still wish that I had it, tucked away somewhere. It was really special to me."

He dragged a hand through his hair. He seemed troubled. Or uncomfortable. Or both.

Then he said, "I think I should check on the horses."

When he stood and stepped off the blanket, Meagan watched him walk away, his tall, broad-shouldered body creating a dark and looming shadow. He was like a gunslinger on his way to a fight.

Garrett used the horses as an excuse to clear his head. He'd spent the last three years, while Meagan was in prison, condemning her for what she'd done, and now he was trapped in a prison of his own making.

This outing was supposed to be an exercise in analyzing her character, not falling for every word she said. Yet everything she'd told him sounded painfully real. Even more disturbing was the memory she and Garrett shared. That stupid flower she'd mentioned. He remembered the moment he'd given it to her and the beautifully fractured way she'd looked at him, as if she needed him more than he could possibly know. He'd pilfered it from the arrangement in the lobby and handed it to her because he'd wanted to make her smile.

He still liked seeing her smile.

Damn, he was losing his perspective. Then again, maybe it wasn't such a stretch that he and Meagan could work toward becoming friends. They'd been drawn to each other from the start.

The sexy stuff wasn't plausible, though. That was definitely off-limits. She was the last woman on earth with whom he should get romantically involved.

He checked on the horses, as he'd said he would. They were fine, of course. But he stayed there with them a bit longer.

Finally, he went back to Meagan. She was sitting in the same spot as before.

"Is everything okay?" she asked.

"It's all good," he replied, even if it wasn't. His thoughts were still scattered.

He rejoined her on the blanket. Then he realized that there was a detail about the day they'd met that eluded him. "Not that this matters, but what kind of flower was it that I gave you?" The bloom she wished that she'd kept. "I don't remember what it looked like." All he recalled was the act itself.

"It was a daisy, and it's funny you should ask, because there's this thing Candy has been studying called the language of flowers, and I'm fascinated by it now, too."

She went on to explain that the type of daisy he'd given her had several meanings—sadness, friendship, protection—all of which felt highly significant to her.

With all the emotional vines that were tangling inside him, he was feeling the significance, too. But he said, "I didn't choose that flower specifically. It was just handy."

"Yes, but it's the one you gave me, the one that was meant to be."

He didn't want to cop to the idea, at least not out loud. "It was just a random thing, Meagan."

She pulled her knees closer to her chest and wrapped her arms around them. "So you don't believe that things can happen for a reason?"

He tried to play down her theory, without squelching it completely. "Sometimes I do, and sometimes I don't."

"Well, whatever it was, whatever the rationale, I think communicating with flowers is a captivating notion."

"It's different, that's for sure." And so was his behavior. He couldn't seem to rid himself of the hunger, the knee-jerk need inside him. He'd never gotten this twisted up over a woman before. If only he could kiss her, just to know how it would feel, just to get it out of his blood.

Was there a flower that meant *forbidden*? he wondered. If there was, he needed to plant them all over his yard, keeping those damned urges at bay.

Meagan said, "Candy is going to carry white roses in her bouquet. And a dyed blue one. They don't exist in nature, so that's why she wants to include them in the ceremony—to represent her unattainable dream coming true. I'll get to carry one, too. I'm going to be a bridesmaid, and Ivy and Candy's dog are going to be the flower girls."

He busted out a grin. "Her dog?"

She smiled, too. "Yogi is a really smart Labrador. I'm excited about the wedding." Her smile fell a little. "I missed my other brother's wedding."

Garrett assumed that meant she was in prison when her oldest brother got hitched. "His name is Kade, isn't it?"

"Yes. He lives in Montana, with his wife and twelve-year-old son. Kade didn't even know he had a son, until a few years ago. Then, when he found out, he got back together with the boy's mother. They're expecting another child now, too."

"Are they going to attend Tanner's wedding?"

"Yes, they'll be there. I was never really close to Kade when I was growing up. There's a fairly big age gap between us. He left home when I was still in elementary school and hardly ever came back to visit. But we've been working on becoming closer now that we both have children."

"That's good." Garrett didn't know much about Kade Quinn, other than he was a renowned horse trainer with celebrity clients who flocked to him. Both of her brothers were successful in their fields.

She released her hands from around her legs. "Tanner said that he wants to meet you. He really appreciates that you gave me a job here."

"Sure, maybe I can meet him sometime. And maybe you can get a bit more acquainted with my foster brothers." It might help to bring Meagan into the fold, for them to see her, too. "Especially since they're such a big part of this."

"Do they hate me for taking the money, the way you used to?"

"I never said I hated you. I just—" he searched for the right words "—hated that you pretended to be something you weren't."

"I'm not pretending now."

He was, he supposed, with how badly he wanted to kiss her. "Just for the record, Jake and Max aren't holding grudges against you. I was more affected by what you did than they were."

"I'd like to see them. It would be nice to be able to apologize to them, like I've been able to do with you."

"Jake used to steal," Garrett said, tossing out a tidbit from the past.

Meagan blinked. "What?"

"He used to shoplift when he was a kid. He was

really messed up after his parents died, and he stole things to fill the hole that was inside him. So, in that respect, he understands how easy it is to do something you shouldn't do."

"Thank you for telling me that." She sighed, a soft sound of relief. "Did Jake ever get caught?"

"Yes, he did, when he was about fifteen. He didn't go to a juvenile detention center, though. He got probation instead, and he learned his lesson, because he never did it again."

She spoke quietly. "And what about Max? Did he ever do anything bad?"

"Not that I'm aware of. But a lot of bad things were done to him when he was a child."

"I'm so sorry. Is Max okay now?"

"Yeah, he's all right. But the hurt and neglect that he suffered is always there, I think, breathing down his neck. You don't get over that kind of pain. He even went on a recent sabbatical, taking time off from everything and everyone. He really is a bit of a mystery. I never really know what he's thinking or feeling."

"You seem like that, too," she replied, reminding him that she'd already put him in the mystery category.

"Yeah, but I'm different from Max. I have a parent who loves me. Jake had a good family, too, even though he lost them. Max didn't have anyone." Garrett gazed solemnly at her. "But without Max, Jake and I wouldn't be as successful as we are today. We all vowed when we were kids that we were going to become billionaires, but it was Max who clung the hardest to the dream, insisting it was possible. He's also the one who made his fortune first, then loaned us the money to start our businesses. The foster children's charity was his brainchild, too. He wanted us to create it together, and it's become vital in all our lives."

"You're good men, the three of you."

"We try to do good things."

"I'm glad the restitution I'll be paying is going to your charity. It would have broken my heart if Ivy had gone into foster care."

"My mom felt broken every time I was separated from her. But it couldn't be helped."

"You're together now."

He nodded. He was grateful that he had the resources to provide for his mother, to give her a life of leisure and pay for the best medical care available. "She used to be a hotel maid. That's what she did when I was growing up."

"That makes perfect sense, doesn't it? With you owning a resort now?" Meagan plucked a long spindly weed that was growing beside the blanket. "We're all a product of our environments, in some shape or form."

"Yes, we are. Products of the lives we've led."

She pressed the weed to her chest, as if it were the daisy he'd given her. "Mine has been mixed up."

"Mine, too." He shuddered to think of how badly he was going to want her as time forged on, with this friendship of theirs on the rise. But instead of yanking it out by its roots, he was allowing it to grow.

Six

The following week, Garrett met with his foster brothers to discuss an upcoming charity event: a big fun-filled, family-style picnic in the park. They were in his office gathered around a conference table, wrapping things up. The rest of the organizers, the people who worked for their Caring for Fosters Foundation had already left. Basically, they'd created the nonprofit to help provide financial and emotional support to foster children.

Garrett poured himself a cup of coffee, his second one that morning. He offered Jake and Max a refill, too. Jake held out his cup, but Max declined, shaking his head.

Garrett silently studied both men. In his heart, the three of them could have been natural-born brothers. They didn't look that much alike, aside from being tall and athletically built, but their bond was strong, as well as the culture they shared.

Jake was the most noticeable, with his trendy clothes, rebellious smile and swooped-back hair. His adoring wife thought that he looked like a Native American version of James Dean. Even as a teenager, Jake had girls flocking around him. He used to say that he was never going to settle down or have children, but he'd eaten those words when he'd gotten his personal assistant pregnant. Marrying her hadn't been easy, though. She'd refused his proposal at first. But, in the end, it had worked out, and Garrett couldn't be happier for them.

Max was a whole other animal. He had been a shy, skinny kid with no social skills and a genius IQ. He hadn't beefed up until he was in his twenties and started hitting the gym. He'd become successful then, too, designing software that had earned him his fortune.

Garrett said to both of them, "There's something I want to run past you."

Max replied, "About the event?"

"No. About Meagan Quinn. You guys already know that I offered her a job and she's been working here, but I was hoping that you'd be willing to meet her. You only saw her around the accounting office. Neither of you have ever really spoken to her." They hadn't attended her sentencing, either. Only Garrett and his mother had gone. "So I'd like to get that cat out of the bag."

"Is this your mom's idea?" Jake asked. "For us to meet her?"

"No, it's mine. But they'll probably get acquainted

soon, too. Mom wants to get to know her." And he couldn't keep them apart for much longer. Nor, he supposed, was there any reason to. "Meagan is a great employee. She works hard, and I'm trying to help her turn her life around."

"So you've forgiven her?" Jake asked.

"I'm doing the best I can, befriending her and whatnot." He chose his words carefully, admitting that they were becoming friends without letting on that he had the hots for her.

Max said, "I'd be willing to meet her, if that's what you want us to do."

Garrett glanced over at Jake. "How about you?"

"Yes, of course. I've always believed in second chances. I have my own delinquent history. But I'm curious about what made the difference for you, especially with how angry you were about getting ripped off. What has she done to convince you that she's changed, besides how hard she works? Because she was a valued employee at the accounting firm, too, before she hacked into our accounts. So why would her work ethic be the deciding factor for you now?"

"It's not just that. I've spent some time with her over the past few weeks, and she's been confiding in me about how messed up she used to be. She explained why she took the money and how sorry she is. She's trying to be a good mother, too, and raise her daughter right. I truly believe that she's being sincere."

"That's nice to hear," Jake said. "And I'm glad you're getting over this."

Yeah, Garrett was getting over the theft, but he was

far from getting over Meagan. "I appreciate that you're both on board."

Jake nodded. "No problem."

Max nodded, too, and moved to stand near the window. Sunlight streamed through the blinds, creating jagged shards of light. Max's favorite sport was shadowboxing, and Garrett often wondered if it was his way of attacking the past and the demons that still lived inside him.

At the moment, Garrett knew the feeling. He wouldn't mind taking a few swings at his own shadow. As much as he wanted to be around Meagan, he was worried about it, too.

What if he got too attached to Ivy? Or what if he never got over his hunger for Meagan? There was a fistful of reasons why he shouldn't be hanging out with her. But, even so, he was determined to follow through on their friendship.

"When should we do this?" Jake asked.

"Do what?" Garrett asked.

Jake rolled his eyes. But he cocked a smile, too. He seemed perfectly relaxed, with his shirtsleeves rolled up and his tattoos artfully exposed. "Meet Meagan. That was what we were talking about."

"I don't know." Garrett hadn't gotten that far, which wasn't like him. Typically, he was a highly organized person.

"Why don't you invite her to the charity?" Jake said. "We'll all be there, and she can bring her kid, too."

"That's a great idea." And something Garrett should

have considered, especially since this particular event was designed for families. "I'll talk to her about it."

"Sounds like a plan." Jake smiled again.

Max didn't say anything, but he'd always been the quietest of the three. He was still standing beside the window in his *Star Wars* T-shirt and time-worn jeans. He wasn't opposed to wearing business attire, in the socially acceptable manner Jake and Garrett typically did. But today he'd shown up in casual clothes, like the nonconformist he sometimes was. Garrett never really knew what to expect of Max.

"Are we good to go now?" Jake asked.

"Sure," Garrett replied. Their meeting had come to an end. "You guys can head out, and I'll stop by the day care later to see Meagan on her lunch hour. She eats with her daughter every day." Already Garrett had become accustomed to Meagan's schedule, keeping her whereabouts etched in his mind.

Meagan and Ivy sat by themselves. The other kids at their table had already finished their lunches and had dashed off to play under the supervision of a teacher's aide.

Meagan and Ivy were still eating. Meagan nibbled on a bologna sandwich, and her daughter was picking at finger foods.

Even though Ivy kept glancing around, she seemed content to stay with Meagan and make their visit last. Meagan, too, was enjoying every treasured second of their time together.

"Mommy! Look!" Ivy pointed to the open doorway that led to the patio. "Garry here!"

Meagan's pulse jumped to attention. Indeed, it was Garrett entering the lunch area. He carried himself in his usual way, like a CEO—strong and polished and confident.

Meagan's daughter wiggled in her seat while Garrett stopped to greet one of the teachers on staff.

"Him see me?" Ivy asked.

"Yes, I think he's here to see you." And to see Meagan, too, but she wasn't going to say that.

Garrett glanced in their direction, and Ivy waved at him. She loved waving at people. He smiled and came over to them.

"Hello, Princess Ivy," he said.

She grinned and stood on the bench seat to welcome him. He sat on the other side of her, steadying her so she didn't fall. Meagan was doing the same thing, and it made her feel as if she and Garrett were Ivy's parents. But they weren't, she told herself. He wasn't Ivy's father. Nor should Meagan be thinking those sorts of thoughts.

The child sat back down and offered him some of her food. He politely refused, but she insisted. So he took a slice of banana and ate it. By now, Ivy was wedged between him and Meagan, and the toddler seemed even more content than she had been earlier. But she was used to having Tanner and Candy as her guardians, so it would stand to reason that she was comfortable being with two attending adults. A couple, if you will. That was her norm. But it wasn't Meagan's. She wasn't accustomed to having a man by her side.

Garrett finally spoke to Meagan. "How are you doing?"

Aside from analyzing herself and her daughter? "I'm fine." She smiled and gestured to her lunch. "Just brown-bagging it."

He glanced at her half-eaten sandwich. "So I see." He accepted a cheese-flavored cracker that Ivy handed him. Then he continued talking to Meagan. "I can't stay long. I have a lot to do today, but I wanted to invite you and Ivy to an upcoming charity event."

"What exactly is it?" She doubted that it was a fancy gala, not if a two-year-old would be coming along.

"It's a picnic at a local park. Lots of kids will be there with their foster families, along with people who are donating to the charity and their families. I'll buy your tickets, so you and your daughter can attend."

"Will your foster brothers be there?"

He nodded. "I just talked to them this morning about it. Do you want to go?"

"Sure." This would give her the opportunity to apologize to his brothers. She also thought a picnic sounded nice. "When is it?"

"Next Saturday." He paused. "Come to think of it, maybe Tanner and Candy can join you. I'll provide their tickets, too. If they come, then everyone can meet everyone."

"What about your mom? Is she included in this?"

He shook his head. "She won't be there. She can't

spend too much time in the sun. But we'll work out another day for the two of you to get together."

Meagan felt a huge weight being lifted from her
shoulders. "Thank you. Meeting her is really important to me."

"Maybe we can arrange it for later this week, if
Mom is feeling up to it."

"That would be wonderful."

In the next quiet moment, Ivy drew their attention,
humming to herself and playing with her food. She
lined up the crackers, making them walk.

Garrett smiled, and so did Meagan. Then he said,
"There are some things about my mom that I'd like
to tell you. Things you should know ahead of time."

She assumed he meant about his mother's illness.
"Just let me know when you want to talk about it."

"Do you want to meet tomorrow, before your shift
starts? I can cook breakfast for you at my house."

Oh, wow. He was inviting her to his castle in the
sky. "You cook?"

He lifted one brawny shoulder in a partial shrug.
He laughed a little, too. "I manage."

"I'd love to join you for breakfast." She'd never had
a man cook for her before. Neil hadn't been that kind
of guy. She searched Garrett's gaze. "Should I bring
anything?"

He looked back at her. "All I need is for you to be
there."

Meagan sucked in her breath. His response sounded
more romantic than it should have. But she knew that

he wasn't inviting her to his house to make out with him. Nothing was going to happen.

Was she secretly hoping that it would? With each week that passed, she was becoming more infatuated with him. Even now, a warm hush had come over them. She couldn't stop staring at him. Neither of them had broken eye contact yet.

Thank goodness they were sitting off by themselves, without any of the teachers nearby to observe them. Ivy, of course, was too young to understand.

Garrett finally glanced away, prompting Meagan to peer off to the side, too. But when he spoke, she shifted her focus back to him.

He said, "There's a security gate before you get to my house, so I'll have to let you onto the property. Just drive up to the gate and push the buzzer."

"Will do." Meagan still hadn't finished her sandwich. She tore at the crust on her bread, and her daughter nabbed it, adding it to the crushed-up crackers she'd been playing with.

"I should go." Garrett stood and ruffled Ivy's hair. "Goodbye, princess."

"Bye, Garry." The child looked up and gave him a handful of crumbs as a parting gift.

He tucked them into his jacket pocket, and she grinned and returned to the mess she'd made.

"See you tomorrow," he said to Meagan. "Sevenish?"

"I'll be there." For a date that wasn't a date, she thought. With a man who was already making her melt.

* * *

The next morning, Meagan arrived at the gate and followed Garrett's instructions to push the buzzer. He buzzed her in, and she drove farther up the hill and parked in front of his house.

She was dressed for work since that was where she would be going afterward. But she hadn't braided her hair yet. For now, it was long and loose and flowing down her back. She'd spent nearly three years wearing a dowdy prison uniform with her hair in a no-frills ponytail. The least she could do was try to look nice, especially when she was on her way to see Garrett. She wanted to be pretty for him.

Nonetheless, she was nervous about this get-together. She'd barely slept last night thinking about it, and this morning when she'd dropped Ivy off at day care, her daughter had given her an extra-special kiss goodbye—as if the child sensed that she needed it.

Meagan took a moment to study the outside of Garrett's beach house–style mansion, with its tree-lined courtyard and enormous picture windows.

But before she could knock or ring the bell, he opened the front door and greeted her. He was dressed for the office. Or sort of dressed for it, she thought. He wore gray trousers and a pinstriped shirt, but it wasn't tucked into his pants. He didn't have a tie.

"Hey," he said.

"Hi," she replied. When she glanced down, she noticed that his feet were bare.

He gestured. "Come in."

She followed him into the entryway, where they

ascended a staircase that led to the living room. From there, he took her into the kitchen.

"Your house is magnificent," she told him. She could see the ocean from nearly every window. Most of his furnishings were made from natural woods. "I love the kitchen." It was decorated in black and white, with an intricately tiled floor. "Everything is so bright and inviting."

"Thank you. Take a seat, and I'll get started on the meal."

"Okay." Meagan sat at a bar-style counter that divided the kitchen from the living room. From her vantage point, she could watch Garrett cook.

He removed a carton of eggs from the fridge. He placed tomatoes on a cutting board, too. He also put potatoes in a colander to be cleaned and peeled.

"Do you need some help?" she asked.

"No, thanks. I've got it." Garrett turned toward her. "Do you want coffee or orange juice? Or both?"

"Juice would be nice." She'd already had coffee this morning.

He poured it from a store-bought carton and set it in front of her. "It's the kind with lots of pulp."

"I like that kind." She took a sip. "I get the sneaking suspicion that you're a better cook than you led me to believe."

"I'm just making eggs and potatoes."

"Yes, but look how good you are at it." He peeled the spuds with a paring knife, working them like a chef. He even had fresh herbs available.

"I'm just fanatical about doing things right."

He did seem like a perfectionist. "I can tell."

She enjoyed watching him move about the kitchen. He remained neat and tidy, without spilling or splattering anything on his shirt. She almost wished that he would, in hope that he would remove it.

Meagan drank more of her juice, trying to cool herself off. She didn't need to be fantasizing about Garrett without his shirt. He was sexy enough, just as he was.

He finished cooking the meal and filled her plate, giving her two poached eggs and a generous helping of pan-roasted, rosemary-seasoned potatoes. The tomatoes had been diced up, drizzled with olive oil and garnished with parsley. There was whole wheat toast, too.

She sat a little more forward in her seat. "It looks fabulous." Normally, she just had a bowl of oatmeal in the morning. Of course when she'd been in prison, she ate whatever they gave her.

He placed a tub of butter and a jar of strawberry preserves on the counter, along with clear glass salt and pepper shakers, paper napkins and sturdy flatware.

He took the bar stool next to hers. "I hardly ever use the dining room table. This is where I usually eat."

"It works for me." She liked that he was seated so close to her. He smelled like cologne. The spicy fragrance mingled with the food he'd fixed. She could've breathed him in all day.

They ate their breakfast, and it was as good as it looked. She smothered her toast in jam, and he spread butter on his.

"Did you tell Tanner and Candy about the charity event?" he asked.

"Yes, and they thought it sounded wonderful, but they can't go. They already have an appointment that day, tasting wedding cakes. If they cancel it, they'll be scrambling to get everything done. The caterer they're using is really busy. They still want to meet you, though. Hopefully, we can arrange it for another time."

"I'm sure we can figure something out."

"Okay, but will you tell me more about the event?" she asked. "And what to expect?"

"Truthfully, I don't know what to expect, other than it's going to be a picnic with games and prizes and sports activities. We've never done anything where the kids themselves would be in attendance. But we thought it would be nice to have something fun for them to do, where the entertainment was created for them. When I was in foster care, a lot of the kids felt like second-class citizens, as if nothing they said or did mattered."

Her heart went heavy. "Did you feel that way?"

"Mostly, I just worried about my mom, but it was hard for me, too, getting bounced in and out of someone else's house every time she got sick. It was a tough and lonely existence, and, without Jake and Max, it would have been even more unbearable."

"How old were you?"

"When I first went into foster care? Twelve. Jake went in when he was twelve, too, and Max had been there since he was eight, but he didn't end up in the same house with us until he was eleven. Jake thought Max was a dork at first, but we all got really close as time went on." Garrett finished his eggs and started on the rest of his food. "Jake's wife used to be a foster kid, too, an orphan like he was. But she handled her grief in more sensible ways. She didn't run wild the way he did."

Meagan could barely comprehend their childhoods. Hers had been bad, but theirs sounded far worse. "Did you all know her back then?"

"No. Jake met Carol a few years ago when she applied to work for our charity. But he hired her as his personal assistant instead. I think he was drawn to her from the start because they suffered similar tragedies."

"What a beautiful thing—them having a baby together."

"It's great to see him so happy."

"Will Carol be at the picnic, too?"

"As far as I know, she will."

"Does she know about what I did?"

Garrett nodded. "Yes, she knows the whole story."

"And now here I am at your house." She stared into his eyes and felt her heart bump her chest. "I never would have imagined it."

"Me, neither." He gazed at her in the same emotional way that she was looking at him. "We've come a long way."

"I like being your friend."

"I like it, too."

Maybe they liked it too much? Meagan felt lightheaded just from being near him. To keep herself from sliding straight off her bar stool, she gripped her fork and ate every last bite of her food. By now Garrett was done, as well.

She helped him clear the dishes, and he said, "Do you want to go outside and sit by the pool?"

"Sure." She assumed that he wanted to finish their conversation out there.

"It's this way." He led her to the back of the house and through a sliding glass door, where his white-bricked patio and kidney-shaped pool awaited. The yard itself was fenced and surrounded by nature.

"It's beautiful out here," she said.

"It's my favorite spot in the house. I have access to it from my bedroom, too."

She glanced in the direction he indicated. She wanted to get a better look, but the blinds on the sliding glass doors were closed, making his sleeping quarters a mystery.

She sat across from him in a wicker chair. "You created a glittering haven for yourself."

"Glittering?"

"In the way the sun hits the water," she clarified, still thinking about his shrouded bedroom. To keep him from noticing her interest in his room, she hurriedly asked, "Where did you live when you were young? When you were with your mom and not in foster care?"

"We had a little apartment above someone's garage. He was a nice old man. He understood how it was for us and never raised the rent or kicked us out when we struggled to pay it."

"Is he still around?"

"No. He died before I was able to repay him for his kindness. I attended his funeral, though. So did Mom, even though she was feeling poorly that day. She's always had her ups and downs."

"Are you going to tell me more about her illness? So I can be prepared when I meet her?"

"Yes, but mostly I want to discuss her association with your mother."

Stunned, Meagan repeated what he said. "Her association with my mother? She knew my mom?" She leaned forward. "When?"

"A long time ago," he replied, while Meagan remained perched on the edge of her seat, waiting for him to expound.

Seven

Garrett noticed how eager Meagan was to hear what he had to say, so he got right to the point, telling her what he knew. "When Mom was researching your background, she discovered that your mother was a member of a Native American women's group that she once belonged to. This particular branch was a sewing circle."

"Was the woman who belonged to that group Mary *Aénéva*-Quinn?" Meagan asked, as if she wanted to be absolutely certain they were talking about the right person.

"Yes. That's her. *Aénéva*. Her maiden name means *Winter Time*." When she nodded, confirming the translation, he said, "My great-great-grandfather's name was *É-hestáseve*. It means *There is Snow*. So that's how my family got the surname Snow." Garrett frowned a little. "I suppose it's strange, isn't it, how your mother's people are Winter Time and mine are Snow?"

"There are a lot of strange things between us, Garrett." She glanced at the pool and then back at him. "How well did our moms know each other?"

"Not well. They only attended a few meetings at the same time. But Mom can tell you whatever you want to know when you meet her. I don't have all the details. I didn't want to know too much about it."

"Why not?"

"Because I didn't used to think it was important."

"But now you do?"

"It's sure starting to seem that way." He couldn't deny this was affecting him now that he'd told her about it. Meagan even looked as if she were battling the urge to cry.

She said, "I nearly fell apart after my mom died. It was so sudden, her heart failure. There was no time to prepare for it." She paused. "But I'm glad that she never saw what happened to me. How I stole the money and went to prison. That would have destroyed her."

"Maybe you wouldn't have done it if she'd still been alive."

"You're right. I'm sure I wouldn't have." The tears Meagan had been fighting gathered in her eyes. "Her funeral was one of the worst days of my life."

Garrett got up and sat in the patio chair next to hers, wanting to be closer to her. "She's at peace, Meagan." In the old Cheyenne way, the souls of the departed traveled along the Milky Way to the place of the dead, where they met with friends and family who'd also passed on.

"I know. But it still hurts."

"I'm sorry." He'd never lost anyone he loved, but he'd lived on the edge of fear, wondering when it was going to happen to him. "When I was in foster care, I used to lie awake at night and worry that my mom was going to die and that I'd never see her again. Then I'd go home and, after a while, she would fall ill again. It was a vicious cycle that never seemed to end."

"You told me before that she had an autoimmune disease. But you never said what it was."

"She has lupus. It's a chronic inflammatory disease. There's no cure for it, but treatment can help control the symptoms. They can range from mild to severe."

"It sounds awful."

"Mom has always been a sickly person. But she has her good moments, too. She hasn't been symptomatic all the time. Even when I was a kid, she was able to work and go places and try to live a fairly normal life."

"So why was she hospitalized?"

"Soon after my twelfth birthday, she took me on a camping trip. She was determined to get out there and commune with nature. She wanted both of us to have that experience. But it backfired, and she got bitten by a tick and contracted Lyme disease. The combination of the Lyme disease and the lupus was too much for her. She got violently ill. Lyme disease can be severe on its own, but for someone with an autoimmune disease, it is even worse."

"No wonder you were afraid that she was going to die."

"It took years for her to recover from the Lyme disease. For her, it became chronic. She couldn't even get out of bed in the beginning. And when she finally got well, she would have relapses." His stomach tightened with the memory. "And even after she recovered, she was still weak from the lupus. It's a miracle that she survived, with the toll it took on her."

Meagan put her hand on top of his, where it was resting on the arm of his chair. "I can only imagine what you went through, seeing her like that."

Her fingertips sent a rush of heat through his body. "I guess it's why I'm still so protective of her now."

"That's understandable." She removed her hand from his and placed it on her lap. "You have a right to protect her."

He wished that Meagan would touch him again. He'd found it soothing and stirring, and he wanted more. So much more. "I'm heavily involved in a lupus foundation. And one for Lyme disease, too."

"Along with running a foster children's charity?" She smiled a little. "You're a busy man."

Not too busy to be enthralled with her, he thought. "I'll let Mom know that we're going to work out a time for you to meet her."

"I really want to hear about her experience with my mother. And I promise I'll be sensitive to her health issues. I won't do anything to wear her out."

"I trust you." In all sorts of ways, he realized.

"Thank you. Hearing you say that is…" She couldn't seem to find the words to express herself.

He understood exactly how she felt. He wanted to express himself by kissing her senseless. But he couldn't.

"It's probably time for me to go work," she said.

No doubt it was. "Maybe we can do this again."

"Have breakfast at your house?"

He looked into her eyes. "Yes."

She gazed into his. "I'd love to come back, anytime you want me to."

He would use any excuse to be alone with her, to satisfy the erotic feeling it gave him. Garrett had it bad— this crazy desire for her. "I'll walk you out."

They got up at the same time, and he escorted her through the house and back down the entryway stairs to the front door. He went outside with her, and they stood in the courtyard of his home.

"Thank you for a lovely morning," she said.

"Was it lovely, Meagan? Even with the heavy stuff we talked about?"

"Yes, it still was." She reached out to hug him.

And *bam*! he was holding her in his arms. Holding her so damned close, he never wanted to let go. He ran his hand down her back, where her long, glorious hair was falling like silk.

"You're a Winter Time woman," he whispered.

"And you're a man called Snow," she whispered back.

"A snowman?" he asked and made both of them laugh. But his silly joke didn't stop the moment from escalating. It only made it seem fresh and sweet. He noticed the scent from the evergreen trees swirling around them.

Meagan remained in his arms, clasped in the hug she'd initiated. Clearly, she didn't want to let go, either.

"You have pretty hair," he said. He was still skimming a hand up and down her back.

"I wore it loose for you." She caught her breath. "I can't believe I just told you that."

He finally released her and stepped back, so he could look at her. "It's okay that you told me." He liked knowing how strongly he affected her.

She bit down on her bottom lip. "I need to braid it before I go to work."

"I can do it for you."

She seemed nervous but excited, too, at the prospect of him doing something so personal for her. "Are you sure?"

"I'm positive." He paused. "Do you have a rubber band?"

"I have this." She reached into the pocket of her jeans and produced a red ponytail holder.

He took it from her. "Turn around, and we'll do it right here." Standing in his courtyard, surrounded by tall trees and big flowering plants.

She presented him her back, and he separated her hair into three sections and began plaiting it into a long, shiny braid. He took his time, doing it carefully. When the job was complete, he wound the ponytail holder around the end.

Meagan turned to face him once again. "Thank you, Garrett."

"You're welcome." Unable to help himself, he skimmed her cheek with his fingertip.

"Just let me know when your mom is ready to meet me," she said, with a slight shiver.

"I will." He didn't ask if she was cold. He suspected that she was feeling all too warm—that her shiver was a reaction to his touch.

She walked to her car, her braid swishing as she moved.

Garrett had no idea how long they could keep this going without being together. Only he wasn't sure what being together would entail.

All he knew was how badly he wanted her.

Meagan adored Garrett's mother. From the very instant they said hello, a bond was formed. The older woman's name was Shirley, and she was kind and gracious and warm.

It was just the two of them in Shirley's penthouse suite. Meagan felt right at home amid the little statuettes of fantasy creatures scattered about. Meagan had always loved fairy tales. As a little girl she'd immersed herself in them.

As for Shirley, she reminded Meagan of a fortune-teller, with her long, graying black hair and colorful clothes. She even had a deck of Native American–themed tarot cards that she was studying how to use. Meagan didn't ask for a reading because Shirley claimed that she hadn't mastered them yet.

They sat next to each other, drinking hot tea from

floral-printed cups. There was a fruit-and-cheese platter on the coffee table, too, ordered from room service.

"Do you have a picture of your daughter that I can see?" Shirley asked.

"I have tons." Meagan smiled and removed her smartphone from her purse. "But this is my favorite." It was the image of Ivy she used as the wallpaper on her phone. Ivy was dressed in her favorite Western outfit and was waving at the camera.

"Oh, my. How sweet she is. Just so beautiful." Shirley glanced up. "She looks like you. And you look like your mother, from what I can recall."

Here it was. The conversation about Meagan's mom. She'd been waiting for this.

Shirley continued by saying, "When I saw you at your sentencing, your last name didn't ring a bell. It wasn't until I researched you later and discovered your mother's maiden name that it hit me. That I once knew a woman whose name translated to Winter Time. Your mother joined the group under her Cheyenne name, not under Quinn."

"When was this?" Garrett had mentioned it had been a long time ago, but the era wasn't clear. "Was my mom even married yet?"

"Oh, yes, she was. In fact, she was pregnant, with her tummy out to here." Shirley formed a large circle with her arms. "She was a lovely lady." A pause, then: "It was about twenty-seven years ago."

"Oh, my goodness. That was me in her stomach."

Garrett's mother gave her a big smile. "Yes, it was you."

Meagan felt a rush of sweet, sweet warmth. "I was there, inside her, when you met. Garrett didn't mention that to me, but I guess he didn't know."

"No, I didn't tell him. Up until now, he hasn't agreed with me about how important it is that I knew your mother. He didn't want to hear the details."

"He said that you and my mother only saw each other a few times."

"That's true. She was a new member, and she only came to two or three meetings. I assumed that she took time off because she was nearing her due date and would be back later. But she never returned. I do remember how easily we talked, though. We joked about her being Winter Time and me being Snow."

Meagan nodded. She and Garrett had joked about the same thing, right before he'd braided her hair with those strong, capable hands. She would never forget the feeling it gave her.

"Your mother talked about her children," Shirley said. "She told me that she had two boys and the one in her womb was a girl."

"Did you tell her about Garrett?"

"Yes, of course. He would have been around five then. He was such a serious little boy."

Meagan tried to get a mental image of him at that age. But it was tough not to think of him as the big, powerful man he was today. "Serious suits him." She waited a beat before she asked, "Did he tell you that I had a baby sister?"

"No, he didn't."

"I was eight when Ella was born. But she died six months later, from SIDS."

"Oh, honey. I'm so sorry."

"After she died, I thought of her as an angel. But she was my mother's little fairy, too. The name Ella means *beautiful fairy*."

"What a pretty name." Shirley reached for one of the fairies in her collection. A tiny winged girl with big brown eyes and blue-black hair. "You can keep this. For Ella."

Meagan clutched the figurine. "Are you sure?"

"Absolutely."

"Thank you." She wrapped the fairy in a napkin and slipped it carefully into her purse. "I'll put it in Ivy's room at my house. She doesn't sleep there yet. She's still spending each night with my brother and his fiancée, but at some point Ivy is going to move in with me. My family thinks it will happen soon, but I'm being careful not to push her before she's ready. It's still hard, though, not having her there."

"I know what you mean. I was lost when Garrett wasn't living with me. But I was too ill to care for him."

"He told me about the camping trip."

"Who would have seen that coming, me contracting another disease on top on what was already wrong with me? But things are so much better now. Garrett and I both weathered it."

"I'm going to meet Jake and Max at a charity event next Saturday. A picnic in the park."

"That will be nice for you. You'll be able to clear the air with them the way you have with Garrett."

Shirley didn't seem to be aware that Meagan and her son were dancing on the edge of desire, with the air getting thicker each time they saw each other.

"Did my mother tell you anything about my father?" Meagan asked.

"No, she didn't. But maybe she would have if we'd gotten to know each other better."

"They had a terrible marriage. But she loved him just the same."

Shirley watched her as the smoke from scented candles perfumed the room. "Do you love the father of your child?"

"Not anymore. I haven't loved Neil since I stole the money." Since she'd met Garrett on that very first day; since he'd given her his handkerchief; since he'd presented her with that long-ago daisy. "But even after I stopped loving Neil, I was still being loyal to him."

"When I discovered that you'd had a baby in prison, it made me so sad for you. Especially when I learned that your boyfriend had washed his hands of it. Then, when I uncovered the connection I once had to your pregnant mother, I just couldn't get you out of my mind."

"Thank you so much for caring about my situation and convincing your son to hire me and help me get paroled. Without you, I wouldn't have such a fulfilling job." *Or be getting so close to Garrett*, Meagan thought. "I love working with the horses. And being near the beach. It's such an idyllic setting."

"I'm glad you're happy working here and that it's

giving you a fresh start in life." Shirley smiled. "Everyone deserves a clean slate."

"Since we've been speaking so candidly, can I ask you something about Garrett's father?"

"If I loved him?"

"Yes." Meagan was curious to know.

"In the beginning, I thought I did. But after he left, all that mattered was the baby I was going to have."

"My daughter is my priority now, too. I'm going to show her the fairy you gave me, and I'm going to tell her its name is Ella."

"I'm glad you came to visit me. We've had such a nice talk."

"Yes, we have." They'd discussed so many vital subjects. Yet the one thing Meagan couldn't mention was how badly she was yearning for Garrett.

The next day, Meagan joined Garrett at his house once again. This time, they'd agreed on six thirty. So she dropped Ivy off at day care, bright and early, and headed for his castle in the sky.

She'd just arrived, and so far all they'd done was embrace. A long, lingering, body-warming hug.

"Are you ready?" he whispered.

"For breakfast?" she asked, just as quietly. "I'm not really all that hungry."

"Then why are you here?"

She shifted to meet his gaze. "To be near you." She softly added, "In your company." She skimmed her fingers down his shirt, wishing she could unbutton it. Once again, he was only halfway dressed for work.

"So I shouldn't cook?"

"Not yet."

He smoothed a hand down her hair. She'd left it unbraided for him. "What should we do instead?"

"You could show me your room." She knew it was a bold thing to say, but she didn't care. She needed to convey her feelings, especially in light of how easily they were touching each other. "I've been wondering what your bedroom is like."

"That's a dangerous thought, Meagan."

"I can't help it." She looked into the depths of his eyes, nearly losing herself in them. They were the deepest, darkest, richest shade of brown with tiny amber flecks that she hadn't noticed before now. "What have you been wondering about?"

"What it would feel like to kiss you."

"That's easy to find out." Meagan lifted her chin, inviting him to satisfy his curiosity.

He hesitated but only for a moment. Clearly, his willpower was on the brink. He tugged her even closer, lowered his head and put his lips warmly against hers.

Holy. Heaven. On. Earth.

Everything inside her went wonderfully weak. The kiss started off soft and slow, like a lone leaf floating in the wind. She lifted her hands and looped them around his neck. By now, Meagan was actually teetering in her boots.

He deepened the kiss, the taste of desire rising between them. She could feel it, overflowing with every sexy swirl of his tongue.

She moaned and asked the Creator to forgive her.

Because anything this good, this hot, this exciting had to be a sin.

"We shouldn't be doing this," he said, even as he kept doing it.

"I know." But she couldn't seem to control her urges any more than he could. Her body was pressed intimately against his.

He tightened his hold on her, his hands looped around her waist. "When I first got to know you, I kept hoping that you would leave Neil, so I could dash in and sweep you off your feet. But you stayed with him, and then I discovered all the craziness that was going on."

The craziness of what she'd done to him and his foster brothers. "I'm sorry."

"No more apologies, Meagan. We're getting past that."

She looked into his eyes as intently as before. The gold flecks were still there, but now she realized it was a trick of the light. A beautiful illusion. "You're sweeping me off my feet now." He was as dashing as any man could be.

He kissed her again and she let the sensation immerse her.

When he stepped back, she asked, "Are you going to show me your room?"

He ran his thumb along her jaw, as if he was memorizing the angles of her face. "I already told you that's a dangerous thought."

"And I already told you that I can't help wanting to see it." She had been memorizing him in her sleep in the hours just before dawn, when she dreamed the hardest. "I've been fantasizing about you since the day you gave me the daisy. I went home that night to Neil, but it was you who was on my mind. You, I wanted."

His voice turned rough, as gravely as she'd ever heard. "Are you seducing me, Meagan?"

Was she? She honestly didn't know. She'd never seduced anyone before. "Before now, all I've ever done was what men told me to do." She'd never been her own woman, speaking her own mind.

"If I take you to my room, all sorts of bad things could result from it."

A jolt of electricity shot through her. "Bad things?"

"I just don't want to take advantage of you."

"How can you be taking advantage of me if I'm seducing you?"

"I don't know." He kept touching her face. "But I don't usually act on impulse."

"Neither do I." Being this impulsive was new to her. "But we don't have to shout it out to the rest of the world." Her instinct was to keep it between them, to let it be theirs, and theirs alone. "No one except us has to know."

His breath rushed out. "A secret affair?"

She nodded. "As far as anyone else knows, we're just friends."

"Are we going to be able to act that convincingly?"

"I was in a school play once," she teased him. "When I was in second grade. It was a Thanksgiving production, and I played one of the Indians."

He smiled. He even laughed. "Now there's a stretch."

She cuddled up to him, close and warm. "I wanted to be the turkey."

"And get eaten?"

"It didn't get eaten in our play. It got to dance around on stage with the pumpkin pie."

He nuzzled her hair. "I love pumpkin pie."

"I'll bake one for you sometime."

"With lots of whipped cream on top?" He ran his tongue along the side of her neck.

This was the most dizzying foreplay she'd ever imagined. "Whatever you want, you can have."

"I want you."

"Then take me." For their secret affair, she thought. For the heat and passion they'd both been craving.

He reached for her hand and squeezed it. "I'm going to show you my room now." He waited a second, as if he was giving her a chance to change her mind.

But she had no intention of doing that. This was exactly what she needed, what she was desperate for.

Garrett took her down the hall, past two guest rooms and into the master suite. The door was already open, and they both stepped inside. He was still holding her hand.

His room boasted cherrywood furniture and maroon-colored accents. The curtains on the glass doors that overlooked the pool were closed, just as they'd been the other day. The paintings on the walls consisted of misty seascapes, and a carefully woven dream catcher, decorated with shiny gold beads and a red-tailed hawk feather, dangled from the headboard. The bed itself was neatly made. Meagan had left hers in a pile of blankets this morning as she'd rushed out the door.

She turned her attention back to him. "Can I unbutton your shirt?" she asked, itching to bare his flesh.

"Only if I can unbutton yours," he replied, moving forward to make the moment happen.

Eight

Garrett was living out a fantasy, right here and now. He was being seduced, but he was part of the seduction, too, taking what he wanted, what he needed.

He'd never expected Meagan to end up in his bedroom this morning, yet here she was—so soft and pretty and willing.

He undid the first button on her blouse. Then the second. Then the third. He stopped there, simply to admire her. By now, he could see the tops of her breasts. Her skin was golden brown, and her bra was white.

She went after his shirt, opening it all the way. And when she placed her hand against his chest, his heart pounded like a shaman's drum.

"Wow," she said, running the tip of an index finger

down the center of his body. "Look at you and your hot-guy abs."

Garrett was too busy looking at her. "You're the hot one." He finished unbuttoning her blouse. He reached around and unhooked her bra, too.

He finished disrobing her to the best of his ability. She had to help, removing her boots and shimmying out of her jeans.

Finally, when she stood before him in her loosened bra and wispy blue panties, he pulled her closer and kissed her. She made a sound that reminded him of something wild. An exotic creature, he thought, in the midst of a forbidden mating. He suspected that she was going to be the most untamed lover he ever had. The most fulfilling, too. Already, it was an intoxicating combination.

Her bra was discarded and so was his shirt. Her breasts were full and round, her caramel-colored nipples hard and pressed against him. He kept her in the tight circle of his arms.

Once again, Meagan made *that* sound, the feral little throat rumbling, and he thought he might lose what was left of his sex-hungry mind. He backed her toward the bed, one step at a time.

"Garrett." She spoke softly. "Shouldn't we pull aside the covers first?"

Details, he thought. But she was right. He wanted to lie upon his cool, crisp sheets with her.

He released her and turned down the quilt. He removed a condom from the nightstand drawer, too. Another detail. A necessity that couldn't be overlooked.

He stripped down to his underwear, and they got into bed. He slipped his hand past the waistband of her panties, and she smiled and slid her hand straight into his briefs.

He was already aroused. So was she. But the foreplay felt good. So damned good. They messed around, rubbing and touching until their undergarments came off.

The early-morning light enhanced her appearance. Meagan's nakedness was breathtaking. Her hair was beautiful, too, fanning across the pillow and tumbling down her body. They hadn't even consummated their union yet, and already he longed to keep her there for the rest of the day. But that was impossible.

To compensate for it, he said, "Will you lie still for me?"

She furrowed her brows. "Why do you want me to do that?"

"So I can taste you." He wanted her to come before he was inside her, to watch her while she mewled and moaned, to drive her decidedly mad.

She didn't refuse his request. She even reached back to grip the rails on the headboard, as if that might help keep her still.

Kissing his way down her body, he treated her with the ultimate care. He took his time, purposely toying with her senses. Her lashes fluttered, but she didn't close her eyes. She watched him as he watched her.

Garrett used his mouth in clever ways, and as he focused on that one little spot, she let go of the headboard and delved all ten fingers into his hair. Lifting her knees, she arched her hips.

So eager. So carnal.

"Do you want more, Meagan?"

"Yes—" she kept her gaze trained on him, her voice going choppy, her limbs quavering "—more."

He kept doing what he was doing, bathing her with lust and intimacy. She was on the verge of orgasm, just seconds away from the first shudder. He felt her resolve, as sure as he felt his own rocking desire. He swirled his tongue, and her hands tightened in his hair.

She came in a feminine fever, shaking against the current and making the erotic sounds he wanted to hear.

He waited until the last shiver receded before he rose up to kiss her forehead. She reacted just as gently, drawing her arms around him.

And holding him romantically close.

Meagan clung to Garrett, giving herself time to recover from the heat shimmering through her veins. It was like glitter, she thought, lighting up her blood.

"You okay?" he asked.

"I'm wonderful." She nuzzled closer. "How are you?"

He pressed his erection against her stomach. "How do I feel?"

Like a man in need, she thought. Ditching her sweet afterglow, she closed her hand around him. She shouldn't be getting so dreamy about him, anyway. This was just an affair, after all. A wild, glorious affair.

"Maybe I better take care of that for you," she said.

"Yeah." He kissed her, his mouth warm and stirring against hers. "Maybe you should."

Meagan stroked him, enjoying the feeling, the hardness of his body, the strength and power he emitted. She didn't ease up, not until she made him bead at the tip. She even collected the saltiness on her thumb, tasting it for her own pleasure.

In the next anxious instant, they rolled over the bed, sunlight streaming in through the windows.

Garrett took the condom off the nightstand and tore into the packet. He put on the protection and entered her.

He pushed deeper, and Meagan wrapped her legs around him.

"Damn," he said, as she squeezed tighter.

She smiled. Obviously, he liked it.

She trailed her fingers along his stomach, tracing his sinfully sculpted abs, unable to keep her hands off of him.

He looked down at the place where their bodies were joined. She did, too. It was a thrilling sight.

They moved in unison, their rhythm slick and ravenous. He shifted his position and rolled over, taking her with him and putting her on top.

She straddled him, and when she tipped back her head so he could pepper her neck with hot little kisses, her hair fell behind her, flowing to her tailbone.

He reached around and grabbed a handful, tugging on the long dark strands and tangling them however he saw fit. His roughness excited her. She almost wished that he would mar her skin, leaving evidence of his kisses. But he seemed to know better than to brand her.

"Have you done this before?" she asked.

"Done what?"

"Been with a woman you shouldn't be with?"

"No. I'm private about who I date, but I don't…"

"Have secret rendezvous?"

He nodded and sought her lips. This particular kiss was terrifying. The kind that left you wanting more than you were capable of handling.

Was he right about what he'd said earlier? Was their affair destined to go bad? She'd stolen from him, this billionaire who lived a quiet and cautious life, and now she was buck naked in his bed. Where was the logic in that?

Nonetheless, she didn't want to stop being his lover. Meagan longed to be with him, to continue what she'd started.

Once the kiss ended, she tried to catch her breath, to slow down and make the moment last. But he was still holding a fistful of her hair, urging her on.

She gave in to the frenzy, riding him hard and fast and becoming part of his thirst for completion.

When he came, she absorbed the slamming shock and pulsing friction. He even growled in her ear.

Afterward, he went into the adjoining bathroom to dispose of the condom and she remained in bed, clutching the sheet. She was still reeling from the force of his climax.

He returned and sat next to her, and she wanted to fling her arms around him and never let go. Of course there was no logic in that, either. However long this lasted, it wasn't going to be forever. But that shouldn't matter. She'd chosen to be with him. She'd acted on her desires. But she wasn't going to allow herself to get attached, at least not in a way that would involve the tattered strings of her heart. Falling for Garrett, any more than she already had, wasn't in her best interest.

Or so she kept telling herself.

"What time is it?" she asked, trying to be brave and free, like an uncommitted lover should be.

"I don't know. I don't have a clock in here."

When he leaned toward her, she waited a beat, thinking that he was going to reach out and hold her. But he didn't. Disappointment washed over her, mingled with a wave of relief. "How do you wake up without a clock?"

"I set the alarm on my phone."

"Where's your phone?" Hers was still in her car.

"In the kitchen. I took it in there before you arrived, when I thought I'd be making breakfast for you. Speaking of which, we still need to eat."

"I can't be late for work." A shot of panic set in. "What if I'm late already?"

"You don't have to be there until nine, and you got here at six-thirty. We haven't been in bed that long."

"Are you sure?" Sleeping with the owner of the resort was no excuse for being late. It would make her feel cheap and dirty, even if she wasn't taking advantage of the situation purposely.

"Yeah, I'm sure." He climbed into his underwear

and then his pants. "You can get dressed and meet me in kitchen. And feel free to freshen up, if you need to."

"Thank you." She worked on calming herself down, on taking a deep breath. "But I still need to be mindful of getting to work on time."

"I know." He resumed his spot next to her. "But I can't help wanting to keep you here."

She smiled, warmed by his admission. Worrying about her feelings for him was foolish. She just needed to go with the flow.

Finally, he headed for the kitchen, and she trailed into the bathroom, carrying her clothes.

Meagan got herself ready. She rebuttoned her chambray blouse, tucked it into her cowgirl-cut jeans and braided her hair, taming the tangled mess Garrett had made out of it.

She entered the kitchen, and he greeted her with a cup of coffee, which smelled heavenly.

He said, "There's cream and sugar on the counter. Sugar substitutes, too, if you prefer those. Oh, and you've got an hour before you need to go to work."

"A whole hour?" She glanced at the microwave clock, confirming the timeline. "Who knew?"

"I did. If you want a repeat performance, we could go back to my room." He waggled his eyebrows. "Or we could do it here. I could lift you onto the sink. Or we could make use of the floor. Or bump and grind against the fridge."

She laughed. "You wish."

"Yeah, I do." Suddenly he didn't look like he was joking around anymore.

Meagan felt the steam rising from her cup. Steam could have been rising from her body, too. She changed the subject to keep herself from mauling him. If they went at it again, she would be late for work for sure. "What are you making for breakfast?"

"I thought I'd throw together something sweet. I've got pancakes in the freezer. I can warm them in the microwave, and we can smother them in syrup."

He made pancakes sound like the sexiest thing ever. And for now, they were. He quickly prepared the meal, and with every bite Meagan took, maple syrup melted in her mouth.

"So exactly when are we going to do this again?" he asked.

She added even more syrup. She couldn't seem to get enough. "As soon as we're both able."

"I'm free on Sunday."

"I might be, if Candy and Tanner can watch Ivy on that day for me. But first you and I need to get through the charity event on Saturday."

"You're right. We've got that coming up." He watched her eat. "We'll be putting our acting skills to the test."

"I don't think I should stay the whole time." Meagan chewed and swallowed, a little more slowly than before. She liked that he was watching her, but he was making her self-conscious, too. "I think it's better if we keep our public appearances to a minimum."

"That's fine. You can arrive late or leave a little early, whichever works for you. But my brothers are expecting you so don't bail out completely, okay?"

"I would never do that." She wanted to make a good impression. "I'll probably be nervous, though, especially now that we're sleeping together."

"I know. It's going to be weird." He moved closer, his face just inches from hers. "But we'll just do the best we can, keeping this secret of ours."

Before she could respond, he kissed her while the syrup was still warm and sticky on both of their lips.

When he let her go, she teetered in her chair and finished her pancakes, devouring every sweet and spongy bite.

Meagan had no idea where Garrett was. She was supposed to text him when she arrived, but she hadn't done that yet. Instead, she strolled through the park, carrying Ivy on her hip.

Along with the barbecue itself, lots of other activities were underway. While a variety of games were being played by some of the younger kids, a group of rebellious-looking teenagers opted for an aggressive match of volleyball. In another direction, Frisbees soared, with humans and dogs alike chasing them. There was a standard playground with slides and swings and such, but a bouncy castle was available, too. On the outskirts of it all was a trackless train, carrying a load of all-aged passengers.

Clearly, there was plenty to do, but Meagan had also brought along a satchel of toys to keep Ivy occupied. She figured they would come in handy when they were sitting still. At the moment, though, Ivy was craning her neck to see everything, pointing to this and that.

Finally, Meagan sent Garrett a text letting him know her whereabouts. She was near a professional face-painting booth.

Garrett quickly replied to the text: Stay there. I'll come get u.

Meagan typed: OK.

It wasn't the most scintillating exchange, but they were both behaving like friends instead of lovers. Adding a sexy emoticon to her message wouldn't do.

"We're waiting for Garrett," Meagan told her child. "We're going to meet his brothers."

Ivy angled her head. "Him brothees?"

"He has two." She wasn't going to say that they'd lived in foster care together or try to explain what that meant. She kept it simple where her toddler was concerned.

"Me no brothees."

No, her baby girl didn't have any siblings. Meagan couldn't even think about more children right now. She was still trying to be the perfect mother to this one. And it wasn't easy, not with her lack of experience.

Feeling far too reflective, she looked at her child's sweet, round face. She'd labored over Ivy's hair today because the two-year-old wanted it in a style that Candy typically fixed for her, and Candy hadn't been home to do it. But Meagan finally created a hairdo that made Ivy happy, using a host of sparkly barrettes. The fussy toddler also wanted to wear her new toy tiara, so that was fastened onto her head, too.

Ivy said, "There Garry!"

Meagan spun around. Dang, but her kid had a knack

for finding Garrett. She was like a bat in that regard, honing in with her "Garry" radar.

As he walked toward them, Meagan's pulse skyrocketed. He moved with masculine grace, his shoulders strong and erect. When he smiled, she thought about how delicious he was in bed.

Ivy reached out to him. Clearly, she wanted him to hold her. Meagan understood just how she felt.

He scooped the child right up. He met Meagan's gaze, but he didn't linger. He played his part like he was supposed to, but their secret was still there, deep in his eyes.

He spoke to Ivy. "Well, look at you, princess. You have a crown."

"Me prinny."

He chuckled and asked Meagan, "Is she saying that she's pretty?"

"No. She's confirming that she's a princess."

"Indeed you are," he said to Ivy.

"Her tiara is new," Meagan told him, noticing how excited her daughter was perched in his arms. "We got it yesterday. She saw it at the pharmacy and insisted that she had to have it. She has some real tiaras that Candy has put away for her. But she isn't allowed to wear those yet."

"Real?" he asked.

"They're not diamonds or anything. But they came from Candy's old beauty pageants, so they're real in that sense."

"Someday Ivy will have lots of diamonds." He bounced her. "Won't you, princess?"

Ivy didn't respond to him. She was too busy watching a rambunctious group of boys who'd come out of the face-painting booth with superhero masks artfully painted around their eyes.

Garrett turned his attention to Meagan. "My brothers already got their food. Carol did also, but she's eating for two. She said it was an excuse to go back for seconds." He smiled and then shrugged, as if his knowledge of pregnant women was limited. "I haven't eaten yet. I was waiting for you and Ivy."

"That was nice of you." She appreciated how courteous he was. "But before we load up on barbecue, can I meet Jake and Carol and Max?" She couldn't eat until that was over.

"That's fine." He gestured to a stretch of lawn past the volleyball courts. "They're out that way. We're not using any of the picnic benches. We brought a blanket and folding chairs for our group."

Meagan noticed that lots of families had done that very same thing. People were scattered all over the grass.

Suddenly Ivy exclaimed, "Me!" and pointed to a little girl with stars and moons on her cheeks. "Me! Me!"

"Do you want your face painted?" Meagan asked her.

Ivy nodded so hard that she looked like one of those toy bobbleheads.

Meagan certainly didn't want to deny her daughter the magic of being made up. "Do you mind if we take a detour?" she asked Garrett. "Then I can meet everyone and we can eat?"

"Sounds good to me." He headed straight for the booth, hauling the little bobblehead with him. "It'll be fun."

They got in line, and Ivy squirmed in Garrett's arms, impatient for her turn.

Thankfully, there was an entire crew of makeup artists doing the work, so they didn't have to wait long. The artists themselves were dressed like fairies, their skin glowing with pixie dust.

Illustrations of the types of designs that were available for Ivy's age range were presented to her. Arms and ankles could be decorated, too. But Ivy didn't know what she wanted. She was more interested in the fairy who was going to paint her.

"Ella," the toddler said, her eyes wide with enchantment. Apparently, she thought that the young woman's costume was real.

A lump formed in Meagan's throat. Ever since she'd shown her daughter the tiny statue that had come from Garrett's mom and told her its name was Ella, Ivy had begun calling all fairies that. Meagan glanced at Garrett and a moment of silence passed between them.

Then Ivy said to the fairy, "Me Prinny Iby."

Meagan translated. "She's Princess Ivy."

The artist smiled. "How about a design with ivy leaves?" She demonstrated where they would go. "And some hearts and diamonds, too?"

Meagan approved of the suggestion. So did Garrett, it seemed, with the way he was grinning at Ivy. But he'd already mentioned diamonds earlier.

The process was quick and easy. Within no time,

Ivy's face was decorated with just the right amount of shimmer to match her drugstore tiara.

The fairy held up a mirror, and Ivy gasped at her new reflection. Clearly, she was delighted with how she looked. Meagan felt great, too, seeing her daughter so happy.

Ivy waved goodbye to the makeup artist, and they were on their way. But Ivy didn't want to be carried anymore. She insisted on walking on her own between Meagan and Garrett and holding both of their hands. When she decided that she wanted them to swing her, she jumped in the air, leaving them little choice but to accommodate her.

Garrett chuckled. "She's got us right where she wants us."

Meagan laughed, as well. Her kid definitely had a superior attitude. "She's the princess, and we're her court."

"So you're the lady-in-waiting and I'm the knight?" He held tight to Ivy's hand and turned his admiring gaze on Meagan. "I'm really glad that you're here with me."

Her heart fluttered. "So am I." She was having a brilliant time, and the day had only just begun.

Nine

As Garrett steered Meagan and Ivy toward his brothers, Meagan geared up for the meeting.

She spotted Jake, looking like a modern-day rebel with his stylishly messy hair and dark sunglasses. His adoring wife, Carol, was an attractive strawberry blonde with a radiant glow. Meagan remembered how it felt to be big and round with a babe in her belly, except that she'd cried through most of her pregnancy, worrying about her child's future.

She noticed how content Jake and Carol seemed. They were seated next to each other, as cozy as could be. It appeared that they'd already finished their lunches and disposed of their plates.

On the other side of Jake, however, was a vacant chair with a paper plate of half-eaten food on it. Meagan assumed it belonged to Max, even if he wasn't anywhere to be seen. The edge of the napkin tucked beneath the plate was fluttering in the breeze, like a bird attempting to take flight—a symbol, perhaps, of Max's elusive personality.

Meagan shifted her gaze. The other vacant chairs were for her and Garrett and Ivy. The one for Ivy was smaller and designed for a child. Garrett had thought of everything.

He made the official introductions. Jake and Carol stood to shake Meagan's hand. They said hello to Ivy, too, and gushed over her painted face.

After the greeting, Meagan spoke directly to Jake, telling him how sorry she was about what she'd done.

He accepted her apology, his manner kind yet casual. They exchanged a smile, and that was that. It was over. She didn't need to mention it to him again. It almost seemed too easy. But she didn't mind. Easy was good.

"What happened to Max?" Garrett asked his brother.

Jake motioned with his chin. "He's over there, talking to Lizzie."

Curious, Meagan glanced in the direction of where Max was. He was engaged in conversation with a beautiful woman, a tall, slim redhead who looked like a socialite, a high-society type Meagan would never come across in the real world. Or a world that didn't involve Garrett and his brothers, she amended.

After a few minutes, Ivy turned restless. She climbed onto Garrett's lap and then onto Meagan's and then onto her own chair. But that didn't last long.

Soon she was sitting on the blanket, dumping her toys into a pile and moving them around. One of them was a monkey with a pink bonnet on its head and a pacifier in its mouth.

Carol asked her, "May I see your baby?"

Ivy inched forward and gave it to her.

Carol rocked the stuffed monkey and said, "I'm having my own baby. For now, it's in here." She patted her ballooning belly. "It's a girl. Like you."

Ivy's little mouth formed a giant O, and she moved closer to examine Carol's stomach. Jake showed Ivy how to glide her hand around to make the baby kick. When it happened, Ivy burst into a fit of giggles, making the adults laugh, too.

"Have you chosen a name for your daughter?" Meagan asked the expectant parents.

Jake replied, "We're going to call her Nita Shivaun. Nita is a Choctaw name so we chose it to represent my family, and Shivaun has Irish origins so we picked that to honor Carol's family. Both sets of her maternal great-grandparents were from Ireland."

"It's a pretty combination." Meagan liked the way it sounded. "What does Nita mean?"

"Bear. We've been getting so many teddy bears as gifts that it just seems to fit. We had a lot of Irish names in mind, but we liked Shivaun because it's the Irish form of Joan, and Carol's mother's name was Joan."

"I named Ivy after a princess in a book I read. Her full name is Ivy Ann."

"She's beautiful," Carol said, studying Meagan's

daughter, as if she were wondering what her own mixed-blood child was going to look like.

Jake's wife returned the monkey, and Ivy placed it on the blanket, putting the plush primate down for its nap. She patted its furry head and gave it a ridiculously noisy kiss. Meagan got all warm and gooey inside, watching her precious girl pretend to be a mommy.

Then, as Max came walking over to them, Ivy looked up and boldly asked, "Who you?"

The returning brother smiled, checking out her glittery ensemble. "I think the real question is, who are you?"

She leaned back on her haunches and repeated what she'd told the fairy. "Me Prinny Iby."

"In that case, I'm Mad Max." He made a funny face. She laughed and mimicked him, scrunching up her features, too. He didn't seem concerned at this point what her actual name might be. Or what his was, for that matter.

But Ivy cared. She said to Garrett, "Him Maddy," just in case he didn't know who his oddball brother was.

"He sure is." He bumped Max's shoulder. They were standing side by side.

Max certainly had an unusual charm about him, Meagan thought, with his longish hair and pitch-dark eyes. Although he was built like a runner, he had some obvious muscle on him. His arms were cut, like Garrett's. No doubt he had hot-guy abs, too. All three foster brothers were tremendously fit.

Max turned to Meagan and said, "I remember seeing

you at the accountant's office, but we never actually spoke." He nodded toward Ivy. "She's rather cool—this sparkly daughter of yours."

"Thank you." She prepared for the apology. "I'm sorry for the trouble I caused. I never should have taken what didn't belong to me."

"It's all right. You did your time. And now you're friends with Garrett." Max glanced at his brother. "He used to keep me from getting my ass kicked when I was a kid. I couldn't defend myself very well back then, and he always came to my rescue."

"You can fight your own battles now," Garrett said.

"Yes, but you were there when I needed it most."

It seemed clear that Max still regarded Garrett as a man who deserved to be honored. Meagan couldn't agree more. She said to Max, "He's been kind to me and Ivy, too."

When a hush came over all of them, Garrett said to her, "What do you think? Should we get our food?"

Meagan nodded, trying to keep a casual air. She wasn't supposed to be admiring Garrett more than was necessary.

He scooped Ivy into his arms. "Come on, princess. It's time for some barbecue." To everyone else, he said, "See you in a bit."

As the three of them headed for the buffet, Meagan glanced at Garrett. "I liked hearing what Max had to say about you."

"I liked it, too. Max doesn't always say what he feels. Sometimes he just stays quiet. He does have a close friend that he confides in, though. Lizzie always lends him her ear."

"Lizzie? You mean the glamorous redhead he was talking to earlier?"

"Yep, that's her."

Meagan couldn't help but wonder precisely what that relationship entailed. "Are they friends the way we're friends?"

Garrett leaned in close and lowered his voice. "If you're asking me if they're sleeping together, then the answer is no."

"How do you know they aren't?"

"Because they've openly discussed *not* being together. They think it'll ruin their friendship if they hook up."

"How long have they known each other?"

"Since their senior year in high school. By then, Jake and I had already graduated and left foster care, so Max was more or less on his own. He tutored Lizzie for one of her classes, which is how they got acquainted. They weren't from the same social circle. She was rich and beautiful and hung out with the popular kids, and he was a poor, skinny nerd who'd never even been to a school dance. But deep inside, they had things in common." Garrett paused. "Inner turmoil. Secrets they shared."

"We're sharing a secret."

He stopped before they reached the buffet, keeping their discussion private. Ivy clung to him, with her painted face shining sweetly in the sun.

He said, "Our secret is different, Meagan. Ours is…"

Romantic, she thought. Sexual. Everything Max and Lizzie's wasn't. "You're right. It's not the same."

After a second of silence, he asked, "Are we on for tomorrow? Did you get Candy and Tanner to babysit for you?"

"Yes." She would be coming to his house, spending a portion of the day with him. "It's all set."

"Where did you tell them that you're going?"

"To a work meeting. I told them that I'm baking a pie for it, too. That people are bringing treats."

He lifted his brows. "Is that going to be a pumpkin pie?"

She smiled. "Why, yes, it is."

"That's awesome." He paused. "But how long is this meeting supposed to last? How long are Candy and Tanner expecting you to be gone?"

"I mentioned that some of us are staying afterward to reorganize the tack room, letting them know I would be gone most of the afternoon."

"Smart thinking."

"Thanks." It was as good a lie as any, and she wanted to make the most of her stolen moments with Garrett, when they could be totally alone.

Unlike now, she thought, as they resumed walking toward the buffet, immersing themselves in the crowd.

Busy as it was, the rest of the picnic went splendidly. After they ate, they took Ivy on a train ride, where she made choo-choo sounds the entire time.

Later, Garrett convinced Meagan to get her ankle

painted. He suggested a blue rose and a yellow daisy twined together. She loved the significance of it, the language of flowers she'd told him about alive in the design.

During one quiet moment, after her ankle was complete, he whispered, "I wish I could kiss you. Here, in front of everyone."

His admission struck her as sweet but frightening, too. Her feelings for him were spinning like a top, and she'd already warned herself to keep their affair in perspective.

So she leaned over and said, "You can kiss me tomorrow when we're alone." She sucked in her breath, trying to keep herself steady. "As much as you want."

On Sunday afternoon, Garrett kissed the daylights out of Meagan—on every part of her body. They'd already had sex. Hot, mind-blowing sex. He wanted to do it again. But for the time being, they leaned against the headboard, balancing plates on their laps and eating the pumpkin pie she'd baked and brought to his house. He'd topped his with a mound of whipped cream, and it tasted delicious, as decadent as a dessert should be.

"I keep thinking about yesterday," he said.

She tucked her feet under the blanket. "In what way?"

"About how tough it was to keep my hands off you." He searched her gaze. "Maybe we should just start seeing each other openly."

She put her plate on the nightstand. Her pie was half-finished. "You want to break our secret?"

"We're both consenting adults." He didn't know how long they could pull this off, coming up with stories, lying to the people closest to them. "With all of this sneaking around, our families might suspect what we're up to, anyway."

"We can always deny it."

"We shouldn't have to deny anything. We have a right to do whatever we want."

She fidgeted with her hands, locking her fingers and then releasing them. "What about public perception?"

"You mean other employees at the resort?"

She nodded. "I don't want anyone thinking that I'm trying to profit from our affair. That I'm using you for your money or trying to find a way to embezzle from you again."

"We've already made our friendship public and no one is accusing you of that now. Besides, there are only a handful of people who even know about the embezzlement, and they haven't been gossiping about it."

"I'll bet they will if they discover that we're lovers." She fidgeted again. "And who knows how long we'll be doing this?"

"Long enough, I hope." He hadn't gotten his fill of her, not by any stretch of his imagination. "I'd be happy to see you—" he raised his fork in the air "—and your pie, every day."

Her voice turned soft. "Really?"

"Yes, indeed." Every day and every night—which sounded excessive, even to him. But he couldn't help it. He wanted to spend as much time with her as he could. "Here's an idea. If you're not comfortable about doing this openly, maybe you can just tell Tanner and Candy the truth. Then you can be with me without having to lie to them anymore." He pressed her to consider it. "Just think about what a relief that would be."

"Yes, but it could create other problems, too. Once Tanner knows what I've been up to, he's not going to like it. He'll probably worry about the effect he thinks it's going to have on me."

"I'm not out to hurt you, Meagan."

She sighed. "I know. But what about my track record and how easily I get attached? I'm already concerned about that."

"You've only had one relationship to speak of. That hardly constitutes a track record."

"It doesn't?"

"No." Not to him, it didn't. "And I'm nothing like Neil, so how bad can it be, getting attached to me?" He wanted her to care about him, just as he was beginning to care about her. "We've got something special going on here."

Meagan sighed again, only it was sweeter this time. "Yes, it's special." She angled her head, her hair spilling to the side. "If I decide to come clean to Candy and Tanner, does that mean you're going to admit it to your mom and brothers?"

"Yes, of course, I'd tell them. I don't think my brothers will say much about it. They don't poke their noses into my love life. Typically, neither would my mom. She rarely even meets the women I go out with. But since this involves you, she might want to discuss it with me."

"Do you think it will concern her?"

"She'll probably just want to be sure that this isn't some quickie thing that's going to hurt either one of us. But you already know that isn't my intention. If I had my way, I'd be taking you out on a proper date for the whole world to see."

She smiled, her skin flushing in the light. "Then what would you do? Get me naked afterward?"

He put his plate aside. He'd devoured his pie and now he wanted to gobble her up, too. "When you put it that way." He leaned over her. "Take a shower with me." He nuzzled her ear. "I want to get warm and sudsy with you."

She caught her breath. "I can't."

Garrett lifted his head. "Why not?"

"Because I can't go home and pick Ivy up with my hair damp and my makeup all washed off. I said I was going to a work meeting, not a pool party."

He skimmed her cheek. "See, now this is why you need to tell your family the truth."

There was another hitch in her breath. "So I can go home all a mess?"

"No. So you can sleep here and let me wash your hair and smear your makeup and do all sorts of sexy things to you." He kept leaning over her. "You should bring Ivy here to stay the night, too. You have a portable crib for her, don't you?"

"Yes, but my daughter isn't even sleeping at my house yet. As much as I want her to move in with me, I'm still new at being her caregiver. Sometimes I think she's ready, and other times I can't be sure. So I'm just tucking her into bed at Tanner and Candy's and waiting until the moment seems right."

Garrett looked into her eyes and saw her fear. "Why? Because you're afraid that she'll reject you if you try it again too soon? Do it this evening. Take her home with you."

"She might throw a fit and cry like she did before."

"And she might not." He placed his hand against Meagan's chest, stilling the choppiness in her breathing. "Isn't it worth the risk?"

"Everything seems like such a risk now. But I guess it always did. I wasn't even sure if I was going to keep Ivy."

Confused by her statement, he set his plate off to the side. "What do you mean?"

"After she was born and I saw how close she'd become to Tanner and Ivy, I tried to convince them to adopt her. I even tried to push them together before they were ready to become a couple, specifically so they could become her parents. I was terrified that I could never be the kind of parent that my daughter needed. Tanner and Candy were just so good with her—"

"You're good with her, too, Meagan. You're amazing, in fact."

"I wasn't amazing in the beginning. I was afraid to hold her or touch her. It was awful, being in prison and not being able to see her every day, so I withdrew from her instead." She pushed a strand of her hair out of her eyes. "I was treated for postpartum depression.

It happens to a lot of women, and it's especially common with new mothers in stressful situations."

"That wasn't your fault."

"No, but plenty of other things were, like how I landed in prison to begin with. If I hadn't stolen the money, I wouldn't have—"

"That's over now."

"I'm still on parole."

Determined to comfort her, to make it better somehow, he kissed her. She moaned beneath him and deepened the kiss, taking what he offered.

Itching for more, he unhooked her bra. It was the kind that clasped in front, making his quest easier.

He rubbed his thumbs over her nipples, making them peak. If only he could lift her up and carry her to the shower. If only they were free to explore each other in every possible way.

"Next time," he said.

She didn't ask him what he meant. But she seemed to understand. If she followed his advice, next time would involve the commitment of her staying the night with him, of being honest about their relationship to their families, of bringing her child to his home, of this being more than just a clandestine affair.

"Doesn't what we're doing scare you?" she asked.

"No." He liked the feeling it gave him. "Being this close to you is exhilarating."

"For me, too, but it's changing so quickly."

"Nothing bad is going to happen."

"That isn't what you said when we first got together."

"I was just trying to protect you then."

Her gaze locked onto his. "And you aren't now?"

"It's a different kind of protection now. It's how a man and a woman should be together. Without lies, without secrets."

"I'm still scared of going this fast." Her words vibrated from her throat. "I've already had too many romantic notions about you as it is."

"Then we'll take it slow."

She shook her head, but she laughed a little, too. "Says who? The big bad CEO invading my dreams?"

He pushed his hand down her panties, and she swallowed the last of her laughter.

"Is that big and bad enough for you?" he asked, shooting her his best lord-and-boss smile.

"I should have known you'd do something like that." She pressed against his fingers, encouraging his dastardly foreplay. "You're making me crazy."

"Likewise." Garrett strummed her, this beautiful lover of his.

While he made her warm and slick, she clawed the sheets. He imagined her leaving nail marks on his bedding.

Or, better yet, on his back.

Anxious to have her, he stripped her completely bare. He ditched his underwear, too, and grabbed a condom.

He plunged deep inside, and when she clawed the hell out of his back, her nails biting into his skin, he couldn't think of anything except the way she came unglued in his arms.

Making him want her more than ever.

Ten

Meagan read a bedtime story to Ivy, just as she'd been doing for the past month. But the difference was that she'd brought Ivy to her house and put her to bed there, as Garrett had encouraged her to do.

And it was working! Ivy was in her crib with a boat-load of cuddly toys, her eyelids getting heavy.

No tears. No fits.

Meagan felt like a real-life mom, and it was the most beautiful feeling in the world. Ivy looked so cute, too, in her pink pajamas and fluffy nighttime hair. She shifted onto her side and pulled one of her stuffed animals closer, as content as a two-year-old could be.

Once Ivy was asleep, Meagan put down the book and came to her feet. She turned off the main light, but she left a nightlight burning. Ivy was afraid of the dark. Meagan had been, too, when she was little. She liked the darkness now, the stars and the moon and the beauty of it.

She exited Ivy's nursery and partially closed the door. Once she was in her own room, she listened for any sounds coming from the baby monitor in case her daughter woke up and needed her. She stayed that way for hours, even though Ivy was in deep repose.

Finally, she gathered her robe and headed for the bathroom, letting her little girl sleep like the princess she was.

Needing to unwind, Meagan filled the tub and added lavender-scented Epsom salts. Then, standing in front of the mirror, she removed her clothes and twined her hair around her head, securing the thick mass with large clips.

While she soaked in the tub, she thought about her dilemma with Garrett. She'd been prepared to keep their tryst a secret. But, for all of the reasons Garrett had pointed out, it made sense to reveal the truth. Still, it was going to be tough for her to admit to her family that she was intimately involved with him. She knew darned well that Tanner wasn't going to approve. What brother would feel good about his jailbird sister sleeping with one of the men she'd ripped off? It just sounded so...

...wrong.

Only it wasn't, Meagan concluded. The affair had been her idea, and she still wanted to be Garrett's lover, as much as ever. It was the speed with which their romance was unfolding that scared her. But she'd already explained that to Garrett, and he'd already told her not to worry about it.

So how wrong could it be?

She stayed in the tub until the water cooled and then slipped on her robe and returned to her room. She had a sudden urge to converse with Garrett, but since there was too much to tell him to put it in a text, she called him. She just hoped that he was available to talk.

When he answered, her heart jumped on the spot.

"What's up?" he asked.

She replied, "All sorts of things."

"Like what?"

She glanced at the baby monitor and smiled. Her child was making soft sounds in her sleep. "Ivy is with me tonight, snuggled up in her crib."

"That's awesome, Meagan. Was it easier than you thought?"

"Yes. She just dozed off, listening to a story I was reading to her, like she does when she's at Tanner and Candy's."

"Congratulations, Mama."

"Thank you." She got into bed and put the phone on speaker. "Know what else? I decided that I'm going tell Tanner and Candy about us." She wasn't going to drag it out, either. "I'm going to do it tomorrow after work."

Garrett's voice wrapped itself around her. "If you do it tomorrow, so will I. I'll talk to my mom and mention it to my brothers, too."

She touched the phone, tracing the shape of it, imagining him on the other end of the line. "We'll have to plan our next get-together at your house soon."

"For sure. I can't wait to be with you again."

She wanted that, too, more than anything. "Are you going riding tomorrow? Will I get to see you at the stables?"

"Unfortunately, I'm going to be tied up in meetings all day. But you can call me tomorrow night, and we can discuss what our families said and how they reacted to our news."

"Okay. Then I guess we should go now." It was getting late, and they both had to work in the morning.

"Night, Meagan. I'll be thinking about you."

"Me, too. About you." In her sleep, in her dreams.

When they ended the call, she removed her robe and got under the covers, with Garrett deep in her mind.

Meagan's talk with Tanner wasn't going well. Her brother was treating her like a child. She wanted to tell him that he wasn't her keeper, but after everything he'd done for her, she couldn't criticize him for reacting the way he was. Still, she wished that he would stop scolding her.

Meagan glanced at Candy in silence. Thankfully, her future sister-in-law was being supportive. Ivy didn't have a clue what was going on. Not only was she too young to comprehend the gravity of the conversation, she was out of earshot, throwing a bouncy red ball down the hallway for the dog to fetch.

"I'm not going to let you keep seeing him," Tanner said.

Before Meagan could respond, Candy came to her

defense. "If she wants to be with him, it's not your place to stop her."

"The hell it isn't." He turned his cloudy gray eyes on Meagan. "Just because he gave you a job doesn't mean he can do whatever he wants with you. You've been through enough with Neil and how he controlled you. You don't need Garrett taking hold of you, too."

"He isn't taking hold of me." Except for her dizzying feelings for him, but that wasn't something she was going to elaborate on to her disapproving brother.

"Are you sure he's not using you?" Tanner asked.

"Yes, I'm sure. I made the first move to become more than friends."

"Dang, Meagan." He frowned. "Why would you do something like that?"

"Because I really like him." And because getting naked with Garrett was like orbiting the moon. It was that special. "You thought he sounded like a nice guy before I told you any of this. You were even interested in meeting him."

"And I want to meet him even more now. If you're determined to keep seeing him, then I think it's important for me to get to know him, too."

"He's a good man, like you are. Ivy certainly adores him." Meagan paused to glance back at her daughter. She was still playing with the dog. "He's going to tell his family about us. He's supposed to talk to his mother this evening, like I'm doing with you. It was his idea for us to tell our families and for me to stop sneaking off to see him and having to lie to you."

"That's good." Tanner calmed down. "That makes

me feel better. Why don't you invite him for dinner here tomorrow night, if he's available to come by then?"

Candy chimed in, "I also think we should invite his mom. After all, she was instrumental in getting Meagan the job."

"That sounds good to me." Tanner looked at Meagan. "Does that work for you, sis?"

"Absolutely." She relaxed, grateful that it was getting resolved. "I'll talk to Garrett about it tonight. I'd planned to call him later, anyway."

Her brother blew out a breath. "I'm sorry if I overreacted. I just want the best for you."

"I know." She reached out to embrace him. "But everything is going to be fine. I'll let you know what Garrett says about dinner. I'll text you after I talk to him."

"Okay." Tanner held her in a big old bear hug, the way he used to do when she was a kid. "And just so you know, I'm proud of the mother you've become."

"Thank you." She hugged him tighter. Without him and Candy, she never could have come this far. "I should probably go home now. It's getting close to Ivy's bedtime, and I need to get her settled in."

Once Meagan was in her own little house, she gave Ivy a bath and got her ready for bed. Like the previous night, her daughter conked out without a hitch, listening to a story. For Meagan, it was a wonderful feeling of déjà vu.

And so was her phone call to Garrett.

"How did it go?" he asked her.

"It was difficult at first, but everything is fine now."

She relayed her experience, explaining how Tanner had come around. She also extended the dinner invitation.

"I'll be there for sure. No doubt Mom will come, too, if she's feeling strong enough to go out. She was doing well this evening when I saw her."

"How did she react to you being with me?"

"She was surprised. She had no idea that you and I were attracted to each other. She was concerned about the outcome, the way I assumed she would be. But I assured her that everything was going to work out fine."

"That's what I told Tanner."

"Then we're on point."

"I'm glad that we don't have to pretend around our families anymore. You were right about coming clean to them."

"And now we can focus on spending time together. Could it get any better than that?"

Her thoughts soared, with visions of romantic days and sensual nights, of touching and holding and kissing. "It's making my heart pound."

"Mine is pounding, too. You're my come-to-life fantasy, Meagan."

"You're mine, too. My dream man."

"Then it's only fitting that I wish you sweet dreams."

"While I wish you sweet fantasies?"

"Definitely."

He cleared the huskiness from his throat. Or he tried to. She could still hear it.

Then, for a stilling moment, he went quiet and so did she, steeped in the heat of each other.

"I'll see you tomorrow at dinner," he finally said.

"You, too," she replied, still lost in the feeling of him.

Garrett's mother accompanied him to Tanner and Candy's house, but she kept stealing glances at him whenever he looked at Meagan. Clearly, Mom was trying to figure out just how serious he was about Meagan. She seemed interested in how close he was to Ivy, too. Garrett did his best to relax and not make too much of Mom's curiosity.

Everyone was gathered around a patio table, drinking coffee or sipping tea, depending on their preferences. They'd eaten indoors and had come out here to enjoy the night air.

Tanner and Candy were kind and caring people, and Garrett found them much to his liking. He sensed that they liked him, too. He and Tanner talked easily. They had a lot in common, with their Cheyenne roots and love of horses.

He'd brought Tanner a bundle of sage as a gift offering, and his mom had given Candy, the future bride, a tall white candle. She'd given Meagan a candle, too, only hers was red and smelled like strawberries. For Ivy, she'd brought a little rag doll dressed in early American Indian garb. Mom was handy with crafts. She'd made the doll specifically for Ivy, just that very morning.

"How are the wedding plans going?" Mom asked Candy. "Are you getting everything done?"

"We're trying, that's for sure. It's been hectic but

fun, too." Candy glanced at her fiancé. "We're having the ceremony at Tanner's stables and riding academy. The land is so beautiful there, with a view of Griffith Park."

"So it's going to be an outdoor wedding?" Mom asked.

Candy replied, "Yes, but since it'll be winter by then, we're going to rent a tent to cover the altar and the aisle, in case it's rainy or cold that day. They make some really pretty ones, so it will add to the ambience, rather than take away from it. We don't need to worry about the reception. It'll be inside." She smiled at Garrett's mom. "I'd love for you to come." Then she turned to Garrett. "And you, too, of course. I'll send invitations to both of you."

"Oh, thank you." Mom spoke up first, accepting the offer. "We would be honored to attend. Wouldn't we, Garrett?"

"Absolutely." He looked across the table at Meagan. He wanted to see her in her bridesmaid's dress, carrying her blue rose. He wanted to see Ivy in her flower-girl finery, too, traipsing down the aisle with Candy's doga dog. "It sounds like it's going to be a spectacular ceremony."

"Thanks. We think so, too," Tanner said, joining the conversation. Ivy was seated on his lap, clutching her new doll. Every so often, though, she would shoot Garrett an impish smile.

The kid was an adorable flirt. Meagan, however, was behaving properly. But he knew how wild she could be in bed, tumbling the sheets with him. Not that he should be thinking about that now, especially in the company of his inquisitive mother.

Earlier, his mom had marveled over a photograph of Meagan and Tanner's mom that was perched on the fireplace mantel, saying that it brought back memories of having known her. Garrett was fascinated by the picture, too. Meagan looked a lot like her mom, with her long, straight dark hair, warm brown eyes and gentle smile.

Before the evening came to a close, Garrett said to Meagan, "Will you give me a tour of your house?" He'd yet to see it, even if he'd caught a faraway glimpse of it out back. "Maybe Ivy can come along, too?"

She smiled. "I'd love to. And I'm sure that Ivy—"

"Me, go." The toddler tried to wiggle out of her uncle's arms.

Tanner laughed. "Okay, little one. Hold on." He helped her down. "Go ahead."

Ivy dashed over to Garrett and reached for his hand. He stood and accepted her tiny palm in his. Garrett's mom was watching him again.

"Do you want to join us?" Meagan asked her. "And see where I live?"

"That's all right," Mom politely declined. "You three go ahead. I'm more than content to stay here and finish my tea."

Garrett understood that his mom didn't want to go trudging across the grass. But he figured that she was trying to give him and Meagan a bit of privacy, too. Nonetheless, he could feel her checking them out as they walked away.

He and Meagan crossed the lawn, heading toward their destination, with Ivy and her new doll in tow.

The area was well lit, with flowers, fruit trees and leafy vines crawling up trellises.

"This is a great piece of property," Garrett said.

"Candy's garden is the focal point. She spends a lot of time tending to it. I've been learning so much from her about plants and flowers."

"Have you been doing some gardening, too?"

"Not yet, but I hope to. Ivy likes digging in the dirt, though." She laughed a little. "So does Yogi. Sometimes she and Ivy get in there and play together."

"What a sight that must be." He laughed, too, and glanced down at Ivy, who was bouncing along between them. "Two loyal companions, with soil-smudged faces, hands and paws."

Meagan smiled. "They are a pair." A moment later, she stopped at the guesthouse and said, "Here we are."

Her home was surrounded by a picket fence. She opened the gate, and Garrett glanced around. Her private yard sparkled, with a fountain out front.

"This is nice." Now he could envision her here the next time they talked on the phone. "It suits you."

"Tanner chose it with me in mind. He used to live in a bachelor pad above his office at his stables. But after I got pregnant and he agreed to take Ivy, he searched for a place that could accommodate all of us. He knows that I like fairy tales, so that's why he thought this guesthouse would appeal to me. It reminded him of the magic cottages in the stories I used to read." She gestured toward the exterior. "It's even called storybook architecture. Initially, it was too small, though. He remodeled it and added a nursery for Ivy."

They went inside. The kitchen was quaint and colorful, and the living room boasted an air of comfort, with a window that showcased the fountain.

Meagan's bedroom, rife with warm woods and brass accents, gave Garrett a thrill, simply because she slept there each night. Now he understood why she'd been so fascinated with his room, too.

Next up was the nursery, which was decorated to the hilt with all sorts of girlishness.

"Mine," Ivy said, letting him know this was where she'd been sleeping these past few nights.

Garrett smiled. "That's a nice bed you have, with all those stuffed animals in it." He pointed to another section of the room. "And look there, you even have your own rocking horse."

Ivy rushed over to the horse, proud to show it off.

"I just got that for her," Meagan said. "It's the first thing I ever bought her on my own, with money from my new job." She moved closer to him. "It felt good to give my daughter a gift that my brother didn't have to pay for."

"Maybe I should give you a raise so you can buy her even more things."

"My wage is just fine."

"Yeah, but the other money that's coming out of it—the restitution…"

"That's fine, too. It's my responsibility to pay it back."

Garrett touched Meagan's cheek, and she lifted her

hand to cover his. Ivy came back over to them, wanting in on the affection. Garrett picked her up, and she put her head on his shoulder.

Meagan gazed at him with admiration. "My daughter has good taste in men."

"And I'm totally into her mother." A romantic impulse came over him, kicking him into high gear. "I want you to go out with me."

"Out with you?"

"On a date. Remember when I mentioned it before, that if I had my way, I would take you out for the world to see?"

She took a step back. "But I'm not ready for that. Telling our families was enough. We're supposed to be taking things slow, remember?"

"Yes, but, in theory, dating is taking it slow. That's what people typically do before they sleep together. We started off backwards."

"I know, but…"

"Men are supposed to take women out, to wine and dine them, to show them how special they are." He looked into her eyes. "And you're far more special than anyone else I've ever been with. Please, Meagan. Let me treat you the way you should be treated."

Her voice cracked. "How am I supposed to say no to that?"

"You're not."

She waited a motionless beat before she said, "Then my answer is yes. But that doesn't mean I'm any less scared."

"Scared of what? Being gossiped about?" He made

the same case he'd made before. "We can't live our lives based on what others think."

"I know." She released a jittery breath. "But that's only part of it."

"And what's the other part? Getting attached to me? It's too late for that. Whatever feelings you have for me, I have for you, too, so what's wrong with exploring them?"

"And dating like normal people? You make it sound so simple."

"It can be, if we let it." He was still holding her child in his arms. But Meagan needed him, too. Intent on quieting her fears, he moved forward to kiss her, a light touch of his lips to hers—proving how good they were together.

And how much he wanted to make this work.

Eleven

Meagan kept changing her clothes, freaking out about what to wear on her date with Garrett. She couldn't afford to buy a new outfit, and she didn't want to ask her brother for the money. Her old clothes weren't out of style, so at least she didn't have to worry about that. Women's fashion hadn't changed that dramatically. But the fancy outfits were from her party days with Neil, and that made her uncomfortable.

Still, she didn't have a choice but to wear something nice. Garrett was taking her on an upscale date: dinner and dancing. She glanced at the clock in her room. She needed to get her butt in gear. He would be arriving to pick her up soon. Thank goodness her makeup and hair were done.

She went for a glittery red minidress, pairing it with

strappy heels. For her jewelry, she chose a sterling silver squash blossom necklace and hoop earrings. She added a turquoise bracelet, too.

Ivy was with Candy and Tanner for the night. Meagan would be going home with Garrett later. She'd already packed an overnight bag.

This date was supposed to give their budding romance a sense of normalcy. But all she felt was anxiety. With each second that ticked by, her excitement mounted. And so did her nerves. This was a turning point in her life. Not getting attached to Garrett was impossible. She was falling for him.

Big time.

But he'd admitted that he was falling for her, too, that his attachment matched hers. And from now on, they would be seeing each other openly.

Heavens, this was scary. Beautifully scary.

Meagan checked her reflection in the mirror one last time as the doorbell rang. She dashed off to answer it, anxious to greet Garrett.

He looked incredibly gallant in a classic black suit, with a lavender-colored shirt and silk tie. No doubt he was sporting all kinds of designer labels. Yet he seemed completely enthralled with Meagan and her little red dress. He just stood there, staring at her. He also had a bouquet of bright yellow gerbera daisies in his hand. She could've melted on the spot.

"Wow," he said. "You're on fire."

"You wouldn't believe how many times I changed."

"Well, you nailed it." He turned over the daisies to

her. "These are for old times' sake, but you probably already figured that out."

"Thank you. They're beautiful." She clutched the bouquet to her chest. "And you're as handsome as ever."

He smiled. "Invite me in?"

"Yes, of course." She was out of practice. Or maybe she'd never actually been on a date like this before. Neil never cared about taking her out, unless it was to hang out at clubs and try to rub elbows with the rich and famous. "Come in, please." She held up the flowers. "And I'll put these in water."

Garrett entered her house, and she searched for a vase, uncertain if she actually had one. Candy had stocked the kitchen before Meagan had moved in.

She found a lovely glass container in the cabinet above the fridge. But it was way in the back.

"I'll get that for you," Garrett offered. He was tall enough to reach the shelf without stretching.

He handed the vase to her, and she arranged the daisies. "When you bring me home tomorrow, these will be waiting for me."

He swept his gaze along her bare legs. "Too bad the flowers from the charity event are gone."

She felt her skin flush. He was talking about the body painting that had been done on her ankle. "It came off in the bath that night."

His gaze roamed over her again. "Are you all set for this evening?"

She nodded. "My purse and overnight bag are in my room. I just need to get them." Before she walked away, she asked, "So where are we going? What restaurant?"

"It's a private dinner club located in the basement of a nineteenth-century home. In the late 1920s and early '30s it was a Prohibition speakeasy run by Sally Sue Milton, the widow whose house it was then. I haven't been there yet. Jake told me about it and sponsored me to join. He said they serve French food and have a live band that plays jazz, blues and Latin ballads."

"It sounds wonderful."

"I thought so, too. I wanted to go somewhere with you that was new to me. And hopefully new to you, too."

"It definitely is." She smiled. "Sally Sue must have been a character."

He smiled, too. "So they say."

"If the club is in the basement where the speakeasy used to be, what do they do with the rest of the house?"

"It's used for private parties and special events. But it's only available to members."

She suspected that it cost a pretty penny to join. His billionaire status was showing, but she didn't want to think too deeply about that. She'd stolen from him, and now she was trying to separate herself from his money, to push it into the background.

But it wasn't easy. He owned a five-star hotel and resort and lived in a house on a hill, overlooking the ocean. She was exposed to his lifestyle every time she saw him. And tonight was no exception.

After she gathered her belongings, he escorted her to the chauffeured limousine that was waiting to take them to dinner.

* * *

Sally Sue's former residence was a fascinating place, and Garrett was glad that he'd brought Meagan here.

Patrons entered through the rear, taking a narrow stairwell to the basement before reaching the original speakeasy door.

The decor in the subterranean space was far more elegant than it had been during Prohibition, but the hidden vibe remained. Sally Sue's picture was on the cocktail menu, and Meagan seemed thoroughly taken with the strangely genteel old broad. Meagan had even ordered a drink named after the woman: a shot of gin served in a vintage teacup. It came with a bowl of sugar on the side that you stirred in yourself. The gin provided by the bootleggers in this area was too bitter for Sally Sue's tastes, so she'd sweetened hers right at the table, sipping it like afternoon tea. In those days, drinking out of teacups was common practice in case of raids.

Garrett chose a Gin Rickey, consisting of gin, lime juice and seltzer. It was a popular Prohibition-era drink referenced by F. Scott Fitzgerald in *The Great Gatsby*. To Garrett, that made it even more interesting. It tasted pretty good, too.

He and Meagan had already nibbled on appetizers, followed by marinated salads, and now they were waiting for their entrées. The band was just starting their set. Later, Garrett would sweep his date onto the dance floor.

He asked her, "Do you know how the term *speakeasy* came to be?"

She sipped her Sally Sue. "No. How?"

"Because it's what bartenders used to say to the patrons, reminding them to speak easy or quietly in public about the illegal places where they were gathering to drink."

"Oh, I like that."

And he liked the way the candlelight was playing off her eyes. Her shimmery red dress was enhanced by the flame, too. "They gave me a brochure about speakeasies when I joined this club."

"Then tell me more about what you learned."

"In order to gain entrance, you would have to say a password or use a specific handshake or a secret knock."

"I wonder what types of passwords they used."

"I don't know. But I doubt they were as complicated as what we're using for our computers now."

She laughed. "Can you imagine if they had to use upper and lowercase letters? And numbers and symbols?"

He laughed, as well. "They would've been standing there all night, trying to remember it." He glanced at the wax melting on the candle and then back at his gorgeous date. "Another interesting thing was how Prohibition changed the drinking habits of women. Prior to that, mostly they just sipped bits of wine or sherry. But then ladies like Sally Sue came along. In came the flappers, too, with their bobbed hair, ruby lips and short, sassy skirts. They flooded the speakeasies, smoking and drinking and being wild."

Meagan held up her teacup. "Here's to those old-time gals."

He joined her, lifting his highball glass. "And to the modern woman here with me tonight."

Her gaze locked on to his. "This is already turning out to be one of the most exciting nights of my life."

His heart punched his chest. "Then let's make it even more memorable and steal a kiss on the dance floor. Public displays of affection aren't usually my thing, but one slow, sexy kiss won't hurt."

"It won't hurt at all." Her delicately painted teacup rattled as she placed it back on the table. "It will probably feel..." She couldn't seem to find the words.

He understood. He couldn't think of anything else to say, either. He swigged the rest of his drink.

"Are you going to get another one?" she asked.

He glanced at his empty glass. "Sure." He signaled the waiter for another Gin Rickey. "But two is my limit." He wanted to be clearheaded for the rest of the night. "How about you?"

"I'm good. One Sally Sue is enough for me."

He suspected that Meagan's lips would taste nice and sweet from the sugar. "Too bad I can't kiss you right now."

"You're too far away." She graced him with a playful smile. "You'd have to climb over the table to get to me."

"Don't tempt me, dear lady. I just might do it." But he didn't, of course. He minded his manners.

His second cocktail arrived, along with their meals. They'd both ordered filet mignon with bordelaise sauce, accompanied by gratin potatoes and porcini mushrooms.

"This looks wonderful," she said.

"Yes, it does." His appetite was plenty strong, for his food and for her. He gazed at Meagan while they ate.

She moaned her appreciation. "This is like dying and going to heaven."

"I'll bet dessert will be even better."

Her eyes lit up. "We should share some pastries."

"Angel wings."

She blinked. "What?"

"If we've died and gone to heaven, then we should have angel wings. They're fried dough covered in powdered sugar and shaped into ribbons. They're thin and crunchy. But, in France, they make a soft variety, too, made with thicker dough. Those are called pillows. They might have that type here since they serve French cuisine."

"Angel wings. Pillows. It all sounds so pretty."

"I want tonight to be pretty."

"It is, Garrett."

"We're going to dance before we have dessert." He didn't want to wait that long to kiss her. The music was already calling to him.

"I'd like that." She swayed a little in her seat. "I wonder what Sally Sue would think of what became of her house."

"I think she would approve."

"I think so, too."

"There was some personal information about her in the speakeasy brochure." Not a lot, but enough to draw

Garrett in. "They say that she loved her husband dearly and mourned him terribly when he died."

"Is losing him what led her to running a speak-easy?"

He nodded. "Supposedly, that was a big part of her motivation. Before he fell ill, he and Sally Sue would frequent other illegal drinking establishments. It was the highlight of their aging lives."

"Now I adore both of them." Meagan made a dreamy face. "Thank you again for bringing me here."

"It's my pleasure." The first of many dates, he thought, with the woman who bewitched him.

Garrett called the waiter over again, only this time he spoke quietly to their server, keeping Meagan from hearing what he was saying.

"What are you up to?" she asked afterward.

"I put in a request for a song."

"How will I know which one it is?"

"Don't worry. You'll be able to tell."

About ten minutes later, they finished their meals, just in time for the band to play "Could I Have This Kiss Forever," a duet recorded by Whitney Houston and Enrique Iglesias.

Meagan snapped to attention. "This is it, isn't it? What you requested?"

"Yes. This is what I chose."

"It's perfect."

He thought so, too. "I figured the band would be familiar with it since they played a few other songs by the same artists."

"Good call."

He stood and approached her. "May I have this dance?"

"You can have as many dances as you want." She looked up at him and whispered, "And kisses, too."

Garrett escorted Meagan onto the dance floor. They moved beautifully together, with the same sensual rhythm they shared when they were in bed.

He kissed her passionately, the lyrics of the song tumbling in his head. He was a teenager when it first hit the airwaves, but he remembered how some of the girls in school used to swoon over it.

Meagan pressed closer, and he slid his hand along the back of her dress, enjoying the feel of her body next to his.

They danced to four mesmerizing songs, and he kissed her during all of them.

"Are you ready for dessert?" he asked.

Yes." She spoke softly. "Angel wings."

"Or pillows," he reminded her.

They returned to the table and scanned the dessert menus that were given to them.

"Both types are available," she said.

"Then let's go for broke."

They agreed on a platter of each, eager to indulge in the powdered-sugar sweetness, no matter how soft or crunchy the pastries were. The waiter brought extra plates, so they could share.

Meagan ate her portion lavishly. "I can't decide which one I like better."

Garrett nodded. "I don't have a preference, either."

"They both remind me of Navajo fry bread but for different reasons." She studied him from beneath her next bite. "Maybe we should make fry bread together sometime."

"Sure. Why not?" He smiled. "I can make it with the best of them. But it's always fun to get at powwows, too. That's another thing we should do together."

She stopped eating. "Since we're going to keep dating and planning events, do you think you could spend some nights at my house?"

"Yes, of course. I'd love to."

"Thanks. It's nice to hear you say that. It will make Ivy happy to have you there. But I'll bring her to your place on other occasions, too."

"I'll be glad to have both of you as my guests." But tonight, it was only Meagan.

She returned to her dessert and then lifted her hands. "I'm making a mess."

So was he but not as much as she was. He gestured to the wet towels that had been provided. "That's what these are for." He went ahead and used his, shooting her a teasing grin. "But you can lick your fingers if you prefer."

"I wouldn't dream of doing that here." She lowered her voice to a discreet level. "But I just might need a shower when we get to your house."

Damn, he thought. Could she be any sexier, reminding him of how badly he wanted to get wet and soapy with her? He leaned in to the table and said, "Imagine that. I just might need one, too."

* * *

Still reeling from their date, Meagan stood in Garrett's luxurious bathroom, removing her clothes. She piled her jewelry on the counter and gazed at her lover.

"Aren't you going to get undressed?" she asked.

"Yes, but not until you do." He was watching her, like a hawk zeroing in on its prey.

Meagan suspected that she was going to get eaten alive, unless she took a big juicy bite out of him first. "This is as far as I go, until you take something off, too."

He cocked an eyebrow at her. "Are you giving me an ultimatum?"

"Yes, I most certainly am." She drew an imaginary man with his broad-shouldered, narrow-hipped body in the air. "It's your turn, Garrett."

"Fine." He took off one shoe.

She stifled a laugh. "Seriously?"

"Yep." He drew an outline that represented her, creating all sorts of curves. He even dotted her imaginary breasts with nipples. "Now you."

Both of her shoes were already gone. "This isn't fair." It was like playing strip poker with half of your clothes already gone. All she had left was her dress and underwear.

"Go on." He prodded her.

Her dress didn't have a zipper. But, thank goodness, she managed to divest herself of the garment without it getting stuck over her head. That wouldn't have been very graceful. She doubted that Garrett would have cared. He was too busy checking out her bra and panties.

She turned in a slow circle, showing him every angle. She'd worn her very best lingerie.

He kept checking her out. "I'm a lucky man."

And she was a lucky woman, being admired by him. "You need to catch up."

"I will," he said, even if he just stood there, looking at her. "In due time."

She moved forward. "Maybe I better help you." She unbuttoned his shirt and then put her hand on his fly. When she toyed with his zipper, he sucked in his breath. She could actually hear air whistling past his teeth.

The game was over. Neither of them wanted to linger over their clothes anymore. He whispered "hurry" in her ear and they both got naked as quickly as possible.

He pulled her tight against him, and they kissed hard and fast.

She thought that he was going to take her, right then and there, against the sink. But he hadn't forgotten their original plan.

He released her and turned on the shower. Meagan stepped inside the stall while he produced a condom from somewhere in the bathroom and joined her.

"You're prepared," she said.

"Always," he replied. "Now you get wet first."

She moved to stand under the showerhead, letting the water pummel her. It soaked her hair and skin. She didn't need to worry about her makeup smearing too badly. Her lipstick was already eaten off, and her mascara was waterproof.

Garrett put his mouth against hers, and they kissed once again. He wasn't playing nice. He was fully aroused and groping the hell out of her.

She tried to get on her knees for him, but he wouldn't let her, telling her that if she went down on him, he wouldn't last.

Meagan found all sorts of power in that. He found power, too, in rubbing his big, hard body all over hers.

He pumped out a handful of liquid soap and lathered every part of her. She washed him, too. But mostly they were just doing it to feel good. This wasn't about getting clean. If anything, it felt dirty. So magnificently dirty. She reached for the condom, but Garrett beat her to it. He already had it in his hand.

He struggled to open it. The packet was downright slippery. She used the extra time to press the front of her body against the back of his. He turned and kissed her, biting at her lip.

Somehow, in the midst of the frenzy, he tore into the packet and put the protection on. Pinning her against the wall, he lifted her up, encouraging her to wrap her legs around him.

Three heartbeats later, he slammed into her.

Steam filled the glass enclosure, rising up to the top. She repeated his name, over and over in her mind. His stomach muscles flexed with every thrust. He was so doggone hot she could have screamed. By the time this was over and he quit manhandling her, she would probably have his thumbprints permanently imbedded on her butt.

She'd never had sex like this before.

Meagan came first. He soon followed, his climax bursting like a volcano. The water kept running, the sound of it shooting past her ears.

Good God.

They slumped into each other's arms, too spent to speak. If he hadn't been holding her, her knees would've buckled.

He rolled his forehead against hers, keeping his hands around her waist. Content to be with him, she closed her eyes, grateful that he wasn't letting go.

Twelve

As the weeks passed, Meagan couldn't begin to count how many times she'd awakened next to Garrett, breathing in the scent of his skin. They saw each other as much as possible, and each moment was as glorious as the last.

On this quiet Sunday afternoon, they were at her house, preparing to take themselves and Ivy out to lunch.

"Let's go to Burbank Billy's," Garrett said.

"Really?" Meagan fastened her daughter's shoes. "That's where you want to eat? A fast-food joint?"

"Heck yeah. I love Billy's. It was my favorite place when I was a kid. And Ivy can play there."

"Me pay!" Ivy said, obviously listening to what he was saying.

"See?" He grinned. "She's totally on board."

"Okay." Who was Meagan to argue with the majority? "I wouldn't mind a burger and fries myself."

"And a milkshake," he added. "It wouldn't be complete without a shake."

"Chocolate?" she asked.

"I'm kind of partial to the strawberry. Their apple fritters are good, too."

She laughed. "Do you realize that all we ever do is eat? And that there's always something sweet involved?"

"Yeah, but nothing is as sweet as kissing you." He reached down and picked Ivy up, twirling her in his arms. "Isn't that right, princess? You like it when I kiss your mama, don't you?"

The toddler nodded. "Garry kissy."

"Yep. Just like this." He moved toward Meagan and planted one right on her lips.

Ivy squealed and clapped.

"Show-off," Meagan said, nudging him away and then pulling him back again. He was darned hard to resist.

They left the house and piled into his truck. He owned several cars, but, on casual outings, he drove a big Ford pickup. He didn't look like a CEO today. He looked more like a California cowboy, with his blue jeans and scuffed leather boots. But Garrett was a chameleon of sorts. He could be highly polished or decidedly rugged, depending on his mood.

Funny, too, how things were moving right along between them. Everyone in their inner circle knew they were together. The other employees at the resort knew, too. Sure, it had caused a buzz at first, but the gossip had died down soon enough. Of course, Garrett had made it known that disloyalty among the ranks wouldn't be tolerated. Even his accountant, who owned the firm where Meagan had stolen money, accepted the status quo. Meagan figured it was probably just for the sake of keeping Garrett as a client. But at least no one was treating her like a leper.

When they stopped at a red light, she turned to look at her lover, studying his handsome profile. Then she said, "I saw my parole officer yesterday."

He glanced over, a slight furrow between his brows. "Did you tell her about us?"

"Yes." She'd been nervous about coming clean to her PO, uncertain what the reaction was going to be. "She wasn't particularly happy about it, but since I'm not breaking my parole by dating you, she couldn't scold me for it. She did express her thoughts, though. Mostly, she was concerned about how it could affect my job if things don't work out between us."

"Your job isn't in jeopardy, Meagan, and neither is this romance of ours." He reached across the center console to put his hand on her arm. "It's just getting started the way it should be."

She smiled, pleased with his answer. They were doing their best to follow a normal path, to enjoy each other's company the way new couples were supposed to.

The light changed, and he crossed the intersection. "You're still my fantasy girl."

And he was still her dream guy. If she could have straddled his lap and kissed him senseless, she would have, even if he was behind the wheel.

When they got to Burbank Billy's, Garrett carried Ivy inside. After their order was ready, they sat at a table in the play area, so Ivy could nibble on her meal with the promise to play once she ate enough of it.

Finally, they let Ivy dash over to the plastic jungle gym, where she climbed inside and poked her head through an oversized hole, along with another little boy about her age.

Meagan was still picking at her food, but Garrett had already finished his double cheeseburger and extra-large fries. He'd drunk half of his shake, too.

"Hungry much?" she asked.

A silly grin stretched across his face. "Yeah, and now I'm going back for an apple fritter. Do you want one?"

"Thanks, but I'll pass." Her stomach would burst apart if she stuffed it beyond its capacity. "But you go ahead and have at it." Garrett and his hot-guy abs. It boggled the mind.

Before he left, he scooted onto the bench seat next to her. "You sure you don't want a fritter?"

"I'm sure." She laughed when he threatened to kiss her, the way he'd done at her house. The exaggerated kisses Ivy liked.

"You don't know what you're missing."

"You can catch me up later."

"I'd rather catch you now." He stole the kiss he was hankering for, leaving her hungry for more.

While he was gone, someone approached the table. Meagan glanced up to see Andrea Rickman, an emotionally troubled, hard-drinking blonde she knew from her old club-scene days with Neil. At the time, Andrea's boyfriend, Todd, had been one of Neil's best buds. For all Meagan knew, Andrea was still part of that reckless circle.

Meagan wanted to run and hide, but there was no escape.

Especially when Andrea said, "I noticed you earlier, but I didn't want to intrude. But now that you're sitting here by yourself, I thought it would be okay to come over and say hi. Truthfully, I didn't even know you were…out." She said the last part with trepidation, obviously referring to Meagan's prison stint.

Meagan hardly knew what to say. "I'm just having lunch." It was a stupid reply but the best she could do under the circumstances.

"Is that your daughter?" Andrea asked, glancing toward Ivy.

"Yes. She's mine." And Neil's, but that went without saying. Clearly, Andrea already knew that.

"That's my nephew she's playing with."

Meagan looked over at the little boy Ivy had befriended. She acknowledged the connection with a quick nod.

Andrea said, "I'm here with my sister." She motioned to a table on the other side of the play area. "She got married about the time you…"

Went to prison, Meagan thought. Andrea kept referring to that. But why wouldn't she? They hadn't seen each other since then.

"I broke up with Todd," Andrea told her. "My sister convinced me to get rid of him. He treated me like a doormat, like Neil did with you. I thought it was awful that Neil didn't want anything to do with your baby. Todd sided with him, of course. But it made me mad. Sometimes I still see him and Todd when I go out, but I never speak to either of them." Silence, then a concerned "Are you doing okay now?"

"Yes, things are good."

"Because of the guy you're with?"

Yes, Meagan thought. But she didn't say that.

Just then, Garrett returned with his apple fritter, and Andrea turned to look at him.

Before things got ridiculously awkward, Meagan said to him, "This is Andrea. She's an old friend of mine."

"Oh, hey. Nice to meet you." He offered a smile. "I'm Garrett."

His name didn't appear to ring a bell. But there was no reason for Andrea to know who Meagan's victims were. The blonde smiled casually at him.

Then she said, "I better go. It looks like my sister is ready to leave. It was good seeing you."

Meagan replied, "You, too."

After Andrea and her family left the restaurant, Garrett asked, "So how old of a friend is she? Did you go to high school with her?"

"I know her from Neil." She repeated everything

Andrea had said to her. "It was weird, running into her like that."

"But you got through it."

Yes, she'd gotten through it. And now she was glad it was over. Ivy came back to the table to climb onto Garrett's lap and drink some of his leftover shake. He gave her a few bites of the apple filling from his dessert, too.

And suddenly everything was right with Meagan's world again, just the way it was supposed to be.

The following week, Meagan was hit with startling news from her brother. Neil had contacted Tanner.

"What did he say to you?" she asked.

"Nothing. He called me at the office, but I wasn't there. So he left a message, asking me to have you call him. He left his number, in case you didn't have it anymore."

She felt weak in the knees. Not the sweet dizziness that Garrett made her feel but the kind that came with fear and nausea. She sat on Tanner's sofa, fighting the sickness coming over her. "Did he say why he wanted to talk to me?"

"No. But I wouldn't trust that jerk if he was the last guy on Earth."

"He probably found out that I'm dating Garrett and wants to poke his nose into it."

"How would he have found out about you and Garrett?"

"I bumped into someone from the past, and I introduced her to Garrett." She explained the Burbank

Billy's encounter. "I don't think she was aware of who Garrett was, though. Nor did she seem like a threat. She never even liked Neil."

"Maybe you should call him to find out what he's up to. If you don't, he might try to see you in person. And we don't need him sniffing around your door."

"You're right. It's safer to call him." Neil knew where her brother lived, and most likely he knew that she lived on the property now, too. "I'll bet he's going to try to use me to get some money out of Garrett."

"Whatever he's trying to pull, we won't let him get away with it."

"Thanks, Tanner. I'm going to go home and call him now. Will you keep an eye on Ivy?" Her daughter had crashed on his floor, with a blanket and a bunch of toys, but she would probably be waking up soon. "I don't want her anywhere near Neil, even if it's just when I'm talking to him on the phone."

"Of course. I'll let Candy know what's going on, too, when she gets home from her yoga class. Are you going to call Garrett and warn him that Neil surfaced?"

"Yes, but first I want to talk to Neil. Then I can give Garrett the full story." Whatever the twisted story was.

Tanner gave her Neil's number, and Meagan walked the garden path to her house, taking in the air, hoping the breeze would help. Her stomach was churning like a vat of spoiled butter.

She went inside and made the call.

As soon as Neil said, "Hello?" her stomach churned even worse, the sound of his voice horribly familiar.

"It's me," she replied. "It's Meagan."

"Well, if it isn't the billionaire's girlfriend."

She fired back, "I'm not anyone's girlfriend." She refused to give him the satisfaction of hearing her admit it.

"Who are you trying to kid? I saw Andrea the other night. She was drunk as usual, stumbling around a club. She gave me an earful about how you'd moved on with some guy named Garrett. She hasn't talked to me since she dumped Todd, and then she comes at me, spouting off about you."

Of all times for Andrea to be brave, Meagan thought.

"Anyway," he said, "I got curious to know if there was even the remotest possibility that the Garrett in question was Snow. And sure enough, I discovered that's who he is. Apparently, you're working for him. And getting cozy with him in burger joints, too."

"What's this really about, Neil?"

"Our daughter," he harshly replied.

Oh, God. He was going to try to use Ivy as his pawn? Meagan's heart skipped a beat.

He continued by saying, "I'm well aware of my mistakes and how I did her wrong. But I want to make amends and be the kind of father she needs."

Meagan would rather die than let him get his hands on Ivy. "That's a load of crap and you know it."

He ignored her accusation. "Have you considered that Snow could be playing a game? Reeling you in to get back at you for ripping him off? I've heard that he has a ruthless streak." There was a long pause. "Unless it's you who's up to no good, trying to take him for whatever he's worth. Either way, I have concerns for our daughter being subject to that kind of environment."

"I'm not—do you hear me? *not*—going to let you see Ivy. So whatever game you're playing, you can end it right now."

"You can't stop me from getting to know my own child. I have rights as a father."

"I'll use the courts to stop you."

"Right. As if you're the poster child for motherhood, dating one of your victims."

"My relationship with Garrett is none of your business."

"If there's nothing shady going on, then why are you getting so defensive?"

"I'm hanging up now. And I meant what I said about you not seeing Ivy."

"Yes, well, we'll see about that."

He ended the call before she could, leaving her in a fresh state of panic, with a flood of tears running down her cheeks.

Garrett rushed over to Meagan's house when she told him about Neil. And now she was shivering like a half-drowned cat.

Garrett took her in his arms, determined to calm her frazzled nerves. She'd taken a long, hot shower before he'd arrived. He assumed that she was trying to wash away the grimy feeling talking to Neil had given her. Her freshly washed hair was still damp, and her tear-marked face had been scrubbed clean.

She peered up at Garrett with red-rimmed eyes. Earlier, she'd told him that Ivy would be staying the night with Tanner and Candy. But he understood that Meagan couldn't bear to let her daughter see her like this.

She said, "Tanner said that if Neil comes around here and hassles me to see Ivy, I should file a restraining order against him. But I don't think Neil is going to do anything to hinder his chances in court. He's not going to make himself look bad in the eyes of the law, not if he expects them to grant him visitations with Ivy."

Garrett smoothed a hand down her hair, catching some of the wet strands between his fingers. "I'll help you do whatever is necessary to keep him away from Ivy. I won't let that SOB come within breathing distance of you or your little girl."

"I think his main objective for now is to figure out exactly what my relationship is with you and use that to his best advantage. But the only way for him to infiltrate our lives is through Ivy."

A stab of guilt punctured Garrett's chest, forming a bloody wound deep in his soul. "If I hadn't pressured you to take our relationship public, none of this would have happened. He wouldn't even know about us."

"It's not your fault." She held both of his hands in hers. "You were right about us dating openly. I don't regret it, Garrett. Not for a minute. But I'm still terrified of the power Neil holds over me. I'm the one who's a parolee, who's dating one of her victims, who struggled with a severe form of depression. Neil has a lot of things to use against me."

"Your postpartum depression shouldn't be an issue.

You recovered from that, and you're an exceptional mother. As for you and me, I'll testify on your behalf that our relationship is good and pure. I'll open up my entire life to them if I need to."

"What about the three counts of embezzlement I served time for? Neil probably doesn't even have a traffic violation. I lied to the police about how he wasn't involved in what I did. I can't go back now and say that he helped me plot those crimes. Sure, the detectives on my case suspected it. But there was no proof of his participation and there never will be. Neil got away with it, and if he gets away with this—"

"He won't," Garrett reiterated. "I'll talk to my attorney and have him recommend someone who specializes in family law. I'll make damned sure that you get the best lawyer money can buy."

Her hands went clammy. "I can't afford someone like that."

"I can."

"I can't let you pay my way."

"So consider it a loan."

"Oh, God." She squeezed her eyes shut, and when she reopened them, they were filled with another round of tears. "I never wanted my relationship with you to be about money."

"It's not about that. What I'm offering is to save you and your daughter from Neil." Garrett would do whatever it took to keep them from getting hurt, no matter what the cost.

Thirteen

Garrett sat on a bench in front of a gourmet coffee shop, located on the boardwalk near his resort. He was waiting for Neil.

Yes, Neil.

Garrett had already consulted his attorney about Meagan's situation, and although a top-notch lawyer specializing in family law had been recommended, Garrett and his advisor had also discussed another alternative. A quicker, easier, cut-and-dry way to keep Neil away from Meagan and Ivy, and that was the route Garrett had decided to take.

He hadn't talked to Meagan about it, though. He wanted to spare her the details until it was over, until he could hold her in his arms and assure her that Neil would no longer be a problem.

So here he was, wishing the other man would hurry up and get here. But Neil, the cocky bastard, was late.

Garrett gazed out at the beach. It was a chilly afternoon, with the wind kicking up sand and the ocean crashing onto the shore.

He'd chosen this spot because it was one of his favorite places on the boardwalk. Meagan had already gotten off work and taken Ivy home from day care, so there was no chance of her happening by.

Garrett shifted his gaze and saw a long-limbed, fair-haired man dressed in jeans and a leather jacket coming toward him. He knew it was Neil. Earlier, he'd checked out Neil's social media accounts to view his pictures, most of which were arrogant selfies. He was younger than Garrett, with blue eyes and pretty-boy features.

Neil plopped down beside him, making a smart-aleck expression, as if he found this whole damned thing amusing. Garrett wanted to ball his hands into tight fists and beat that smug look right off his face, but that wasn't on the agenda. He needed to stick to the plan.

"So did Meagan give you my number?" Neil asked.

"No. I got it on my own."

"Does she even know that you arranged this meeting?"

"No," Garrett said. "And you're not going to say anything to her about it. In fact, after today, you're never going to speak to her again."

"I'm not?" Neil raised his eyebrows. "And how do you propose to make that happen?"

"By giving you a shitload of money to stay away

from her and Ivy." Garrett had no intention of beating around the bush. He wanted to get this done and over. "My attorney already drew up a document, where you'll be relinquishing all claims to Ivy. After you sign and accept the money, for all intents and purposes you will no longer be her father." Garrett slanted him an icy glare. "Not that you are, anyway, not where it counts. But legally, you'll be giving up your parental rights. There's also a nondisclosure agreement you'll need to sign, prohibiting you from speaking about this for the rest of your miserable, soon-to-be rich life."

"How rich?" Neil slyly asked.

Garrett removed a slip of paper from his pocket with the figure written on it.

Neil's head nearly swiveled on his neck. "Did you bring the documents with you?"

"They're at my attorney's office. I'll text you the place, day and time. But you'll need to bring your own attorney to read the legalese to you."

"I can read. I can—"

"Just bring a lawyer." Garrett wasn't going to let this conniving prick come back later and say that he'd been railroaded into this. Or that he didn't understand the fine print. Or any other cock-and-bull thing he might try to concoct.

"If I sign a nondisclosure agreement, what am I supposed to say to my friends?"

"About your sudden windfall? I'm sure you'll come up with a plausible story to tell them." Considering what a good liar he was.

Neil jerked his chin. "This better not be a scam to

make me look bad in court later. Like you're filming this and are going to present it as evidence. Because that will create trouble for you, too, bribing me the way you are."

Garrett cut his reply to the quick. "This isn't a bribe. It's a business arrangement, and you'd do well to know the difference."

"Okay, hotshot. But what if I don't accept the terms you're offering? What if my attorney thinks I should hold out for more?"

"Then the deal is off." He shoved the paper with the figure on it back into his pocket. "And I'll never offer you another dime again."

"You've got it all figured out."

"Yes, I do." And Garrett wasn't wavering. "So you've got two options—take it or leave it."

And he was certain that Neil would take it, since Garrett was giving the lowlife exactly what he wanted.

Monetary wealth in place of a sweet, beautiful child.

Meagan was at Garrett's house, sitting in a patio chair beside his pool with her hands clutched to her chest, listening to him tell her about the deal he'd orchestrated.

He finished with "I spoke to Neil yesterday about it, and he signed the papers this morning. It's over. You won't be seeing or hearing from him ever again."

Speechless, she just sat there, his news swinging like a razor-edged pendulum, slicing her emotions in two. Neil was out of the picture, gone from her and Ivy's lives.

She could have wept from gratitude, cried from absolute joy. Except for the other part of it...

Garrett had given Neil money. He'd gone behind her back, using his power and influence to "fix" her problems, and that made her feel like his cheap-hearted mistress. An ex-con sleeping with a billionaire. A woman who would never live an honest or upstanding life.

When she finally spoke, her vocal cords rattled. "You shouldn't have done that, Garrett."

He gave her an incredulous look. "What?"

"You shouldn't have paid him off. You shouldn't have even approached him without talking to me first. The decision should have been mine."

"But I wanted to spare you the trouble of being involved. I just wanted to come to you and say that it was done." He shook his head. "And why does it matter, as long as he's gone?"

"Because I wouldn't have agreed to your method." Her hands were still pressed to her chest, where a hollow cadence beat its way to her throat. "I just couldn't have gone through with something like that."

"You wouldn't have taken the easiest and quickest method of getting rid of Neil?" He looked at her with accusation in his eyes. "Why the hell not?"

"For so many reasons." She hated that this was turning into a showdown. That she couldn't speak her mind without him taking offense. "But mostly because I can't stand the thought of you giving him money and putting me and Ivy in the middle of it. As scared as I was about facing off with Neil in court, I would have stood tough when I needed to, fighting my battles the legal way."

"There was nothing illegal about the way I handled it," he shot back.

"Then why does it feel so criminal to me? I was already uncomfortable about hiring a pricey attorney and borrowing the money from you to pay the fees. That was already weighing on my self-esteem. But this goes beyond anything I could've comprehended."

"So what are you saying? That I did something that damaged you?"

"Not purposely. But you made a decision that wasn't yours to make. You controlled a portion of my life that wasn't yours to control."

"Like Neil used to do?" Garrett scowled at her. "How am I supposed to feel with you comparing me to him?"

"I wasn't doing that. I wasn't—"

"Yes, you were."

Meagan struggled to remain as calm as this discussion would allow, to keep from breaking down in confused and frustrated tears. "You're putting words in my mouth."

"Do you know how long a court battle could have taken? Or the anguish it would have caused you and your family?" His scowl deepened. "Neil would have put you through the wringer, trying to finagle a way to make a buck out of being Ivy's dad. He would have been there at every turn, using you and your daughter to get to me."

"So you beat him to the punch? Why can't you at least try to understand my perspective?"

"And do what? Apologize for paying that bastard

off? No way." He got out of his chair, pacing the poolside pavement. "No effing way will I ever be sorry for that."

"You rewarded him for his bad behavior."

He stopped pacing, turning sharply to face her. "At least you and Ivy will never be burdened by him again."

"I'm so incredibly glad he's gone." She couldn't pretend otherwise. "And for that, I'll be eternally grateful to you. I know you meant well." God help her, she did. "But, on the flipside, you can't just go around paying people off to make things easier for me. I already told you that I didn't want our relationship to be about money."

"I did what I thought was right."

"But it wasn't right for me. I've been working tooth and nail to be a better person, to complete my parole, to meet my obligation and pay the restitution I owe. But now I owe you for getting rid of Neil, too." And that was a debt she would never be able to repay. "I'm not like you, Garrett. I'll never earn that kind of money, not in an entire lifetime."

"Get real, Meagan. You don't owe me anything."

"So I'm just supposed to accept you paying him off?" She fought the tears she refused to cry. "How can I condone that?"

He tugged a hand through his hair, his movements tense, choppy. "Maybe we should stop seeing each other. Maybe being together isn't going to work."

His dismissal cut her to the core, and so did the stubborn pride in his eyes. Instead of trying to understand, instead of coming to an emotional compromise—he was ending what they had.

"I don't want—" *To lose you*, she thought.

He went as still as a statue. "You don't want what?"

She didn't reply. If she gave in, there would be nothing left of her, of the independent woman she was trying so hard to become.

He remained as motionless as before. Then he roughly said, "This doesn't change the status of your job. I'd never take that away from you. It's yours, for as long as you want or need it."

She held her breath, her lungs ballooning with air, filling her with pain. "Ivy is going to miss you."

"I'm going to miss her, too." He cleared his throat. He was speaking softly now. "I don't think I should stop by the day care to visit her, though. That might confuse her, if I'm not with you anymore."

"Will you still come by the stables when I'm there?"

"Yes, I'll still see you when I go riding. I just won't be able to…"

Touch her and hold her and kiss her? His unspoken words tore a hole through her heart. Neil was gone, but so was her romance with Garrett. That wasn't supposed to be the solution.

"I need to go," she said. She couldn't stay here a millisecond more. It was killing her to be this close to him.

Hurting worse than anything she'd ever known.

Meagan went home and told Candy what had transpired. But by now she was too distraught to keep her emotions under control, bursting into intermittent tears and drying them with the tails of her shirt. "I swear, I didn't mean to push him away."

Her brother's fiancée gently replied, "You were just being honest with him about how it affected you."

Meagan drew her knees up to her chest. She and Candy were in the garden, seated on the grass. Ivy was inside, playing with Tanner and the dog. Meagan was surrounded by family, yet she felt so horribly alone. "His intentions were good, but he shouldn't have taken his protection that far. Of course, that's what he does. Protect people, I mean. When he was young, part of his motivation to become wealthy was to have the means to take care of his mother. And when he was in foster care, he stood up for Max when he was being bullied."

"Those are amazing qualities for someone to have."

"Yes, they are." Garrett was the most amazing man she'd ever known, right up until the moment he'd let her go. "Before today, he kept reassuring me that it was okay for us to explore our feelings, and that he was as attached to me as I was to him."

"I'm sure he still he is, Meagan."

"Attached, but detached." She rubbed her swollen eyes. "I can't fathom not having him by my side. It's going to be unbearable waking up every day, missing all of those wonderful moments I used to spend with him."

"I wish I could make it better for you."

Only Candy couldn't do that. No one could. But the worst of it, the most difficult part, was the fear that was unfurling: the knee-jerk panic that Meagan had already fallen in love with him.

She didn't want to feel that way, but she didn't know how to stop it. Nor could she bring herself to admit it out loud. Yet it existed in the recesses of her broken heart, turning her life inside out.

It was painful. Too much to grasp.

"This shouldn't have happened," she said, talking in riddles, trying to make sense of it. "Not now."

Candy plucked at a blade of grass. "I'm sorry he hurt you."

"What am I going to say when Ivy starts asking me where Garry is? How do I tell her that he won't be coming to our house? Or that we won't be going to his? She loves curling up in front of the TV with him. He watches princess movies with her." Fairy tales, Meagan thought, with happy endings. "But I have to be strong for myself and my daughter. To make my own decisions, to be my own woman. That's what I was trying to explain to Garrett, what I was trying to make him understand."

"Maybe something will happen that will bring him around to your way of thinking. Or maybe you could discuss it with him again after the dust settles."

"It's a big issue for us to resolve." And now that she was fighting the ache of loving him, it seemed even bigger. "I can't make the first move. If I do, then I'll go back to being the girl I was when I was with Neil, desperate for a man's approval."

"However this turns out, at least you're free of Neil and any future damage he could've caused."

Because of Garrett, Meagan thought. Even as mixed

up as all of this was, he'd acted on her behalf, protecting her and Ivy like the fallen hero he'd become.

Garrett plastered an upbeat smile on his face, faking his way through the happy occasion. Jake and Carol's beautiful new daughter had arrived today, and the hospital room was filled with love and cheer, with flowers and balloons and teddy bears.

Brightness. Life.

Carol was in bed, cradling the blanket-wrapped infant, and Jake was seated on the edge of the mattress, beaming like a first-time father should be. Max was there, too, in full-fledged uncle mode. If only Garrett could feel their joy.

Five grueling days had passed since he'd ended his romance with Meagan, and he battled the loss every second of every hour. He hadn't even seen her at the stables, as he'd claimed that he would. He'd been taking his horses out when he knew she wasn't there, sparing himself the ache of being in her company. He'd tried to do right by her and Ivy, but Meagan had made him feel like an interloper instead. Were his actions wrong? Had he overstepped his bounds? He was too damned lost to even know.

He gazed at his foster brothers, cooing over the baby. He hadn't told them about his breakup. He hadn't told his mom, either. He'd been keeping it inside.

Finally, Garrett moved closer to the bed. "Can I hold Nita?" he asked. He'd yet to cradle his niece, to press her against his heart, to absorb her newborn warmth.

Jake proudly replied, "Of course." He removed the child from his wife's arms and the transfer was made.

Garrett looked down at the baby's chubby-cheeked face. She'd inherited Jake's golden skin and thick dark hair. Her eyes were shaped like his, too, except they were green like her mother's.

The baby made a cute and comical noise, a tiny snort of sorts, and Garrett smiled, this time for real. "Hello, funny bear," he said. "I'm your uncle Garry."

The infant gazed at him. Or he thought she did. For all he knew, she was staring into space, trying to get those Irish eyes of hers to focus.

Now he longed for Meagan and Ivy even more. He wished they were here, sharing this experience with him. "She's perfect," he said to both of her parents. "You created a wonderful little person."

He returned Nita to her mother. He couldn't hoard a baby who wasn't his.

When it was time for Nita to nurse, Garrett and Max left the room, leaving Jake alone with his wife and child.

Once they were in the hallway, Max said, "I'm going to grab some chow at the cafeteria. Want to come?"

"You go ahead. I'll just get a granola bar or something out of a machine."

"Then I'll see you in a bit." Max shot him a quick wave and headed for the elevator.

Garrett scanned the choices in the vending machines but decided to skip it. He was too preoccupied to eat. So he went to the nearest waiting room, an open area with pastel-painted walls and floor-to-ceiling windows.

He was the only person there, alone with his scattered thoughts.

About five minutes later, he spotted his mom heading toward him, clutching a small gift bag. He stood and went over to her.

"I didn't know you were coming by today," he said. "I thought you were going to wait until they took the baby home."

"I was, but I changed my mind. So I called my driver, and he brought me over. I'm just so excited to see little Nita."

"She's a doll. But Carol is feeding her now, so we're just biding time until we go back in. Max went to the cafeteria."

"That's fine. I'll wait here with you."

Garrett resumed his seat with his mom by his side. "What did you get the baby?" he asked.

"I made her a pair of moccasins. I've been working on them for a while."

"I'm sure her parents will love them." He didn't doubt the love and care that had gone into them. "You're going to be a terrific great-aunt. Nita is going to adore you."

"She's going to adore you, too. Just the way Ivy does. You've got a good thing with Ivy and her mommy."

His chest crumbled, right along with his heart, but he didn't say anything. He merely sat there, mired in his loss.

"Are you okay?" his mother asked, catching sight of his discomfort.

He tried to shrug it off. "I just have a few things on my mind."

"Do you want to talk about it?"

"Really, it's all right. I can handle it."

She tucked a strand of her gray-streaked hair behind her ear. "Are you sure?"

No, he thought. He wasn't. But he didn't want to burden anyone with his problems, least of all his mom. Yet keeping it to himself was starting to tear him apart, too.

Looking for an emotional escape, he glanced out the window that was behind him. The view was of the parking lot.

He turned back around to face her. "If I tell you, you might agree with Meagan and think what I did was wrong, too."

"Whatever it is, I promise I won't judge you, Garrett."

He relayed the entire story, and she listened patiently, her gaze trained on his.

Afterward he asked, "So what do you think?"

"Truthfully, my opinion doesn't matter. What happened is between you and Meagan. But I do think that there might be some other factors involved, things you haven't even considered." She adjusted the gift bag on her lap and the paper made a crinkling sound. "For example, why did you do it? Why did you go to such an extreme measure to get rid of Neil?"

"I already told you, to get him out of their lives."

"Yes, but why?"

"Because I couldn't bear to see Meagan and Ivy get hurt."

"Again, I'm going to ask you why."

Troubled by her tactic, he pulled back. "Why are you grilling me like this?"

"Because I want you to think about it. Not off the top of your head like you've been doing, but all way down—" she leaned forward, pressing a gentle fist to his gut "—from your soul."

Garrett flinched, feeling as if he'd just been shot. Suddenly, he knew exactly what she meant. Or maybe, fool that he was, he'd known it all along and just hadn't dealt with it properly. But the truth was there now, like a lead bullet piercing his already-frayed spirit. A gaping hole, he thought, that provided the answer.

For every lovelorn thing he'd done.

Fourteen

Eager to see Meagan, Garrett left the hospital. Since she was at work, he drove to the stables, preparing to unleash his heart.

But would she forgive him? Accept him? Love him? Want him? There was only one way to find out.

As soon as he arrived, he parked his truck, climbed out of the vehicle and searched the barn for her.

She was in the tack room, by herself, cleaning a stack of leather bridles. She was so focused on her task that she didn't even know he was there, standing in the doorway, watching her.

She looked pretty, as always, in her rough-hewn clothes and long shiny braid. But she looked troubled, too. Because of him, Garrett thought. The last time they'd talked, he hadn't listened to her reasoning. He hadn't respected her thoughts or feelings. He'd flown off the handle instead, destroying the bond they'd built.

And now he was trying to fix what he'd broken.

"Meagan." He said her name softly, so as not to startle her.

She glanced up, and their gazes met from across the space that stretched between them. He entered the room and closed the door behind him. But he didn't crowd her. He kept a cautious distance.

"What I did was wrong," he said, getting straight to the soul of it. "I can't lie and say that I'm sorry Neil is out of the picture. But I had no right to pay him off without your permission, and for that I am sorry."

She set aside the bridle she'd been oiling. In a bucket at her feet were the bits and chains that went with it.

She said, "I've missed you, Garrett. I've been waking up every day, thinking about you, wishing I could see you. And now you're here."

Yes, he was here and had a lot more to say. "Jake and Carol's baby was born today, and she's just the sweetest thing. And when I held her, it made me miss you and Ivy and everything we had. Everything I ruined."

Meagan seemed to sense that he wasn't done talking, so she remained quiet, allowing him to say his emotional piece.

He continued, "I didn't tell my brothers what was going on with you and me. I'd been keeping it inside. Then my mom showed up at the hospital and noticed that I seemed out of sorts. It wasn't easy, but I admitted it to her." He paused to ask, "Did you tell your family?"

"Yes," she replied. "Mostly, I confided in Candy. But my brother knows what's going on, too. They feel bad that I've been hurting, but they're grateful to you that Neil is gone."

"I don't want to be responsible for your pain anymore. I don't want to be *that* guy. Because that would make me like Neil, and I'm not him. I love you, Meagan. And I love your daughter. That's no excuse for what I did, but it's the reason I was so desperate to get rid of Neil. I couldn't stand for him to hurt you anymore than he already had, but then I ended up hurting you, too. I behaved horribly afterward, letting my pride tear us apart." He shook his head, chastising himself for it. "You were right to hold your ground, to show me the kind of woman you are." He took a step toward her. "The woman I love."

She moved forward, too, until she was walking straight into his arms.

"Does that mean you love me, too?" he asked, needing to be sure.

"Yes, I love you." She confirmed her feelings, saying it out loud, letting the words soothe him. "You just made me happier than I've ever been."

Garrett held her close. "I want to keep making you happy, Meagan, to marry you and adopt Ivy. But I won't push you to make it happen. The time has to be right for you."

She looked up at him. "I want to be your wife more than anything and have you become Ivy's father, too.

But I do want to wait awhile. It's important to me to finish my parole and pay my restitution first."

"I understand." He truly did. He wasn't going to take her for granted. He'd nearly lost her, and he was never going to let that happen again.

She stayed in his arms. "Can I still work at the barn after we're married? I like it here."

He ran his hand down the length of her braid. "You can do whatever you want."

"Can we give Ivy lots of brothers and sisters?"

"Absolutely. I've always wanted a houseful of kids." He envisioned his home the way it should be, filled with love and joy. "Will you come to my house later and bring Ivy with you?"

"So we can tell her that I'm going to marry you and you're going to become her daddy?" Meagan smiled. "We'll be there with our bags packed."

Garrett grinned. "So you're going to move in with me, are you? This future family of mine?"

"If you'll have us."

He kissed her, giving her his answer, this forever lady who would someday be his bride.

On the day of Tanner and Candy's wedding, Meagan marveled at every splendid detail. The colors they'd chosen were silver and gold. There were bits of blue, too, like the dyed rose in Meagan's hand. She waited in the wings, preparing to walk down the aisle with the other bridesmaids. But, for now, she was watching Ivy.

Her daughter toddled toward the makeshift altar,

with Yogi by her side. Ivy's dress was a puff of ruffles and lace, trimmed with delicate bows. She wore a crown of posies in her hair and sequined shoes. She was the cutest, brightest flower girl, hanging on to the dog's rhinestone leash.

Ivy kept glancing around at all the people. When she spotted Garrett sitting in the front row, she dropped the dog's leash and ran over to him.

Meagan's heart melted on the spot. Both man and child were the loves of her life.

Ivy climbed onto Garrett's lap, where she decided to stay. Yogi, the brilliantly trained Labrador, continued to the altar by herself.

Tanner stood like the elated groom that he was, dashing in his traditional tuxedo and white rose boutonniere. Ivy waved at him, and he smiled and returned her greeting.

When Meagan's turn came to walk down the aisle, she took the arm of the groomsman she'd been paired with—her oldest brother, Kade. His wife and son were seated in the same row as Garrett, along with Garrett's mom. Shirley was already becoming a grandmother to Ivy.

The ceremony continued, and, finally, when the bride's song was played, everyone stood and turned to view her.

Meagan got a lump in her throat. Candy was more beautiful than she'd ever been, with her mermaid-style gown hugging her curves. She wore a single strand of pearls around her neck, and her hair was swept into an elegant twist and decorated with gilded combs. She carried a cascading white bouquet with a single blue rose in the center.

The vows Tanner and Candy took consisted of words they'd written themselves. During her oath Candy mentioned the unattainable dream that had come true, referencing the special roses she'd chosen for herself and the other women in her bridal party.

Meagan's eyes misted. Someday, in the near future, this would be her and Garrett, standing at an altar, professing their love and devotion.

By the time the reception was underway, Meagan was seated next to her man, enjoying a delectable meal. Garrett's foster brothers had been invited to the wedding, too, so they could meet Meagan's family.

Jake and Carol brought their new daughter. She was exactly a month old today. They didn't plan to stay long, considering how young she was, but they wanted to make an appearance and show her off. She was an adorable baby, all gussied up in pink.

Meagan was looking forward to having more children, not just for her and Garrett but for Ivy, too. So she could become a big sister. Already, she was crazy about little Nita. Earlier, she'd peered adoringly at the baby in her carrier.

At the moment, though, Ivy was chattering up a storm with Max. She'd grown quite fond of Max, or Maddy, as she called him.

After the meal, Garrett asked Meagan to dance and,

as they swayed to the music, he said, "This is a wonderful gathering."

"Yes, it is. Everyone we love is here."

"Including each other."

She looked into his eyes. Truer words had never been spoken. "You're my heart, Garrett Snow."

"And you're mine, Meagan 'Winter Time' Quinn." He spun her around. The song had changed to an up-tempo tune.

They glanced over and saw that Max was dancing with Ivy, lifting her high in the air and rocking her back and forth.

"Me, fun!" she said.

They laughed, charmed by her enthusiasm. She was enjoying herself on this merry occasion, and so were they. Life was good, Meagan thought.

Beautifully, magnificently good.

After Garrett and Meagan got home from the wedding, they put Ivy to bed. She conked out right away, exhausted from the festivities. Garrett loved that Meagan and Ivy were living with him now. He loved watching his little princess sleep, too. On nights like this, his house really had become a castle in the sky.

He tucked the blanket around Ivy. "She had a big day."

Meagan nodded. "We all did."

"Are you ready to turn in, too?"

"With you? Anytime."

They went into his room—their room—and he unzipped her dress, a softly draped gold-tone gown with a jeweled neckline.

"You look gorgeous in this," he said. "But you look just as ravishing out of it." Her undergarments were sexy as sin. Wisps of silk and lace. If he wasn't careful, they would tear apart in his hands.

She smiled. "You're quite handsome yourself."

Garrett removed his tie and draped it over a chair. He'd discarded his jacket earlier. "I've been thinking about our wedding."

"I've been thinking about it, too, and how amazing it's going to be. But I still want to wait until my parole ends and my restitution is paid."

"I know." He wasn't going to hurry her. They'd made an agreement, and he was holding up his end of the bargain. He walked over to the dresser. "But I do have something to give you." He opened the top drawer. "I bought it a few weeks ago, but I kept it hidden in a safe until today."

She came closer to see what her gift was, and he handed her the ring-sized box. Then he said, "I want us to be officially engaged."

She flipped open the velvet-lined box and gasped. He'd shopped specifically for the diamond, choosing it for its flawless clarity and vivid blue color, much like the flower she'd carried today.

"Oh, my goodness." She looked as if she might cry. "I don't know what to say."

He'd designed the ring as a classic solitaire, simple in its elegance, assuming it was the timeless style she would prefer. But he'd still given her a piece of jewelry that spoke volumes. The diamond was as rare and beautiful as she was. "Just say that you'll wear it."

"Yes, of course, I will. It's stunning. More perfect than I could have ever imagined." She slipped it onto her finger, where the stone dazzled against her skin. "I'm going to have to use gloves when I'm at work to protect it."

"My stable-hand bride. I'm so proud of who you are."

"And I'm so honored to be your fiancée."

"I have a diamond for Ivy, too. It's a princess-cut pendant for her to wear on the day of our wedding. And anytime she wants to wear it after that, too."

"You're going to spoil us, Garrett."

"I can't help it. I'm excited about having you as my wife and Ivy as our daughter."

"Me, too." She kissed him, soft and sweet and slow.

He guided her to bed, and they finished removing their clothes. He caressed her bared body, and she arched and sighed. He knew just where to touch her, indulging in foreplay that pleased her.

She knew what he liked, too. She used her hands and her mouth, giving him wicked thrills.

Her hair was fixed in a long, wavy style, leftover from the wedding, with little crystals pinned into it. While she did wild things to him, he toyed with her ladylike coiffure, scattering the pins.

Finally, when he couldn't wait any longer, Garrett reached for a condom. Someday, when they were ready for more children, they wouldn't be using protection. But for now this was part of the process.

Once he was inside her, he pulled her tight against him, savoring the naked intimacy. He'd been waiting a long time to feel this way, to care about someone this much.

The sex overflowed with heat and passion. But so did the love. Garrett and Meagan were right where they belonged.

Together in every way.

* * * * *

Don't miss the first
BILLIONAIRE BROTHERS CLUB *book*
from Sheri WhiteFeather!

WAKING UP WITH THE BOSS.

Available now from Harlequin Desire!

And Max's story is next!

COMING NEXT MONTH FROM

HARLEQUIN™ *Desire*

Available February 7, 2017

#2497 THE HEIR'S UNEXPECTED BABY

Billionaires and Babies • by Jules Bennett

A billionaire investigator and his assistant vow to bring down a crime family even as they protect an orphaned baby from the fallout—and give in to their undeniable attraction! But the secrets she's keeping may destroy all they've been working for...

#2498 TWO-WEEK TEXAS SEDUCTION

Texas Cattleman's Club: Blackmail • by Cat Schield

If Brandee doesn't seduce wealthy cowboy Shane into relinquishing his claim to her ranch, she will lose everything. So she makes a wager with him—winner take all. But victory in this game of temptation may mean losing her heart...

#2499 FROM ENEMIES TO EXPECTING

Love and Lipstick • by Kat Cantrell

Billionaire Logan needs media coverage. Marketing executive Trinity needs PR buzz. And when these opposites are caught in a lip lock, *everyone* pays attention! But this fake relationship is about to turn very real when Trinity finds out she's pregnant...

#2500 ONE NIGHT WITH THE TEXAN

The Masters of Texas • by Lauren Canan

One wild, crazy night in New Orleans will change their lives forever. He doesn't want a family. She doesn't need his accusations of entrapment. Once back in Texas, will they learn the hard way that they need each other?

#2501 THE PREGNANCY AFFAIR

Accidental Heirs • by Elizabeth Bevarly

When mafia billionaire Tate Hawthorne's dark past leads him to time in a safe house, he's confined with his sexy, secret-keeping attorney Renata Twigg. Resist her for an entire week? Impossible. But this affair may have consequences...

#2502 REINING IN THE BILLIONAIRE

by Dani Wade

Once he was only the stable hand and she broke his heart. Now he's back after earning a fortune, and he vows to make her pay. But there is more to this high-society princess—and he plans to uncover it all!

REQUEST YOUR FREE BOOKS!
2 FREE NOVELS PLUS 2 FREE GIFTS!

HARLEQUIN®

Desire

ALWAYS POWERFUL, PASSIONATE AND PROVOCATIVE

YES! Please send me 2 FREE Harlequin® Desire novels and my 2 FREE gifts (gifts are worth about $10). After receiving them, if I don't wish to receive any more books, I can return the shipping statement marked "cancel." If I don't cancel, I will receive 6 brand-new novels every month and be billed just $4.55 per book in the U.S. or $5.24 per book in Canada. That's a savings of at least 13% off the cover price! It's quite a bargain! Shipping and handling is just 50¢ per book in the U.S. and 75¢ per book in Canada.* I understand that accepting the 2 free books and gifts places me under no obligation to buy anything. I can always return a shipment and cancel at any time. Even if I never buy another book, the two free books and gifts are mine to keep forever.

225/326 HDN GH2P

Name   (PLEASE PRINT)

Address   Apt. #

City   State/Prov.   Zip/Postal Code

Signature (if under 18, a parent or guardian must sign)

Mail to the **Reader Service**:
IN U.S.A.: P.O. Box 1867, Buffalo, NY 14240-1867
IN CANADA: P.O. Box 609, Fort Erie, Ontario L2A 5X3

Want to try two free books from another line?
Call 1-800-873-8635 or visit www.ReaderService.com.

* Terms and prices subject to change without notice. Prices do not include applicable taxes. Sales tax applicable in N.Y. Canadian residents will be charged applicable taxes. Offer not valid in Quebec. This offer is limited to one order per household. Not valid for current subscribers to Harlequin Desire books. All orders subject to credit approval. Credit or debit balances in a customer's account(s) may be offset by any other outstanding balance owed by or to the customer. Please allow 4 to 6 weeks for delivery. Offer available while quantities last.

Your Privacy—The Reader Service is committed to protecting your privacy. Our Privacy Policy is available online at www.ReaderService.com or upon request from the Reader Service.

We make a portion of our mailing list available to reputable third parties that offer products we believe may interest you. If you prefer that we not exchange your name with third parties, or if you wish to clarify or modify your communication preferences, please visit us at www.ReaderService.com/consumerchoice or write to us at Reader Service Preference Service, P.O. Box 9062, Buffalo, NY 14240-9062. Include your complete name and address.

HD15

A billionaire investigator and his assistant vow to bring down a crime family even as they protect an orphaned baby from the fallout—and give in to their undeniable attraction! But the secrets she's keeping may destroy all they've been working for...

Read on for a sneak peek at
THE HEIR'S UNEXPECTED BABY
by *Jules Bennett*, part of the bestselling
BILLIONAIRES AND BABIES series!

"What are you doing here so early?"

Jack Carson brushed past Vivianna Smith and stepped into her apartment, trying like hell not to touch her. Or breathe in that familiar jasmine scent. Or think of how sexy she looked in that pale pink suit.

Masochist. That's all he could chalk this up to. But he had a mission, damn it, and he needed his assistant's help to pull it off.

"I need you to use that charm of yours and get more information about the O'Sheas." He turned to face her as she closed the door.

The O'Sheas might run a polished high-society auction house, but he knew they were no better than common criminals. And Jack was about to bring them down in a spectacular show of justice. His ticket was the woman who fueled his every fantasy.

Vivianna moved around him to head down the hall to the nursery. "I'm on your side here," she told him with a soft smile. "Why don't you come back this evening and I'll make dinner and we can figure out our next step."

Dinner? With her and the baby? That all sounded so… domestic. He prided himself on keeping work in the office or in neutral territory. But he'd come here this morning to check on her…and he couldn't blame it all on the O'Sheas.

Damn it.

"You can come to my place and I'll have my chef prepare something." There. If Tilly was on hand, then maybe it wouldn't seem so family-like. "Any requests?" he asked.

Did her gaze just dart to his lips? She couldn't look at him with those dark eyes as if she wanted…

No. It didn't matter what she wanted, or what he wanted for that matter. Their relationship was business only.

Jack paused, soaking in the sight of her in that prim little suit, holding the baby. Definitely time to go before he forgot she actually worked for him and took what he'd wanted for months…

Don't miss
THE HEIR'S UNEXPECTED BABY
by Jules Bennett,
available February 2017 wherever
Harlequin® Desire books and ebooks are sold.

If you enjoyed this excerpt, pick up a new
BILLIONAIRES AND BABIES *book every month!*

It's the #1 bestselling series from Harlequin® Desire—
Powerful men…wrapped around their babies' little
fingers.

www.Harlequin.com

Whatever You're Into… Passionate Reads

Looking for more passionate reads from Harlequin®?
Fear not! Harlequin® Presents, Harlequin® Desire and
Harlequin® Blaze offer you irresistible romance stories
featuring powerful heroes.

♦HARLEQUIN *Presents*.

Do you want alpha males, decadent glamour and jet-set
lifestyles? Step into the sensational, sophisticated world of
Harlequin® Presents, where sinfully tempting heroes ignite a
fierce and wickedly irresistible passion!

♦HARLEQUIN *Desire*

Harlequin® Desire novels are powerful, passionate and
provocative contemporary romances set against a backdrop of
wealth, privilege and sweeping family saga. Alpha heroes with
a soft side meet strong-willed but vulnerable heroines amid a
dramatic world of divided loyalties, high-stakes conflict and
intense emotion.

♦HARLEQUIN *Blaze*

Harlequin® Blaze stories sizzle with strong heroines and
irresistible heroes playing the game of modern love and lust.
They're fun, sexy and always steamy.

Be sure to check out our full selection of books
within each series every month!

Love the Harlequin book you just read?

Your opinion matters.

Review this book on your favorite book site, review site, blog or your own social media properties and share your opinion with other readers!

Be sure to connect with us at:
Harlequin.com/Newsletters
Facebook.com/HarlequinBooks
Twitter.com/HarlequinBooks